SECRETS ARE DEADLY

By S. P. MOWRE

FIRST EDITION

This is a work of fiction. Unless otherwise indicated, all the names, characters, businesses, places, events and incidents in this book are either the product of the author's imagination or used in a fictitious manner. Any resemblance to actual persons, living or dead, or actual events is purely coincidental.

Table of Contents

1. ON THE RUN

In the middle of the night, the watch on his wrist vibrated waking him up. It was paired with his home intruder alert. Someone had come for Mike Wilson. He rolled off the bed grabbing his .45 while thumbing the safety off. He looked at the silent alarm panel. The guest bathroom window on the other side of the house showed open. He wondered how far inside they had gotten. Grabbing his "quick" bag from his closet, he lifted up the decorative tile near the foot of his bed and dropped under the house, pulling the floor shut.

The easy thing to do was to kill them. The hardest was to run. Wilson opted for easy, if for nothing else to send a message to any that would follow – and they would. He was going to save Maria; then he was going to kill the people that had ordered her disappearance.

He quickly crawled through the 75' tunnel he had dug months ago and exited near his garbage can in the alley. The damn garbage truck had packed the exit down so it delayed his getting out by another minute longer than he had timed it. While putting on his shoes, a flash-bang grenade went off in his bedroom. It was not as loud as he thought it should have been. Maybe it was new high tech stuff. Looking over the fence, he could see two shadows moving in his room. In less than a minute, he had assembled his sniper rifle and began taking them down. The only noise was the sound of his bedroom glass window breaking as his Teflon bullets pierced the stillness of the night.

In another two minutes, he had packed up and was walking down the alley with a silenced .22 in his hand. There had to be surveillance somewhere. Ah, there it was, at the street corner. They had sent a woman. Well, who would call the police on a woman parked in a neighborhood talking on her cell phone? Only this one was trying to watch too many mirrors and not doing a very good job talking.

Moving quickly, Wilson half jogged and half crawled. He opened her door and raised his .22. He had misjudged her. This one was quick and holding an automatic in the other hand. She fired twice. The first round went wild and the second found its target, burning across his left side before he was able hit her in the throat with the butt of his gun.

Survival kicked in and she clawed at no one and fought for air. He picked up her gun and asked her if they had come for him. She may have nodded but then again she was moving her head in every direction. Funny thing when people could not breathe; nothing else mattered. She was too busy trying to live as he shut the door. It did not happen. Before he left, he used her cell phone and called its last number to say come get the bodies.

He instinctively grabbed his side when the pain ebbed. His hand came up bloody and it made him even angrier. It was time to bring in some help. He needed to get his wound looked at and then he needed to find a place to stay. He hurried over a couple blocks and started down the street when he saw the small house for sale. If it was empty, it meant safety.

Wilson scouted it out and entered via a bedroom window the realtor must have left open for air. There were no clothes in the closet or the large dresser. All the cupboards were empty in the kitchen except for a few dishes. The main level consisted of one bedroom, the small kitchen, a small sitting room, a tiny bathroom and no basement. He washed the blood off his hand and dried his hand on his pants. The layout, the lace curtains with nightshades screamed Grandma's house. Every room had furniture. There was a narrow stairway the led up to an attic. It also had two windows.

Its single attached garage held a well-used 1965 four-door Ford with the keys in the ignition. The garage floor was clean. He was home. Tomorrow he would buy it, all of it if he could. A few security changes would be required, even though they would never come looking so close to his last home.

He closed and locked the window that allowed him entry. In the bathroom cupboard, he found a large towel and ripped it into strips to hold a smaller towel as a pressure bandage. It would have to do; he was exhausted. The bed looked inviting, but Wilson thought it might be safer to sleep in the car. He climbed into the back seat, placed his quick bag on the floor and rolled down the window about one inch. Within minutes he was asleep.

2. HELP ARRIVES

Wilson woke up to hear two car doors shut. He scrambled out of the Ford and into the front room just in time to see a woman wearing a gold realtor jacket, walking around the front of her car. He ran back, pulled a long-sleeve shirt from his bag, and buttoned it over the one with dried blood. Wilson grabbed the nearest Realtor's card from a table near the door, glanced in the wall mirror to see someone that had not shaved and with tousled hair, before exiting the front door.

"Who are you?" she asked.

Glancing down at the card in his hands, Wilson replied, "Oh, I guess Steve Richards didn't tell you. I just bought this house."

"I'm Denise Harrington, the listing agent, and no, he didn't. I wouldn't have brought a client out if I knew a sale was pending."

"Forgive my manners I'm Mike Wilson."

"Mr. Wilson, you look like you just woke up. Did you stay here last night?"

"Well, I'm embarrassed to admit it, but the deal hinged on my spending one night. You know, to make sure it didn't have a loud furnace or loud neighbors."

"Hmmm. Do you mind if I call Mr. Richards? He should have called me."

"No, please do. In fact, let me make the call and get Steve on the phone." Before she could object, Wilson used his trac-phone to call the number on his card. Lucky for him, Richards answered.

"Hi Steve, this is Mike. Look, I absolutely love the house and as I said last night, I will be paying cash."

With Denise Harrington watching him, he became more animated than his words and walked to the side of the house out of sight and her hearing.

"Look, Steve, you don't know me, my name is Mike Wilson. Denise Harrington is at 617 North Glen with a client, but I got here first and I want this house. I will pay cash today and throw in another $5,000 for you if you go along with my story of our meeting last night. I told her I spent the night here with your permission to make sure I liked it."

There were a few seconds of silence before Richards spoke.

"Let me get this right. You stayed last night in Denise's grandma's house on North Glen?"

"Yes, that's correct."

"And, after spending the night, you are going to buy that house today, with a cashiers check for $179,000 – plus $5,000 cash after the deal is signed, for me. Is that right?"

"Yes sir, but I want the car and all the furniture for that price since I am paying cash."

"If you can be at my office in one hour, put Denise on the phone."

Wilson walked around front and handed Denise Harrington his phone. She was talking to her client and neither one looked very happy. She took the phone, listened to what Steve had to say, and politely scolded him perhaps for the benefit of her client, before saying goodbye.

She returned the phone saying, "Well, Mr. Wilson, I guess you have yourself a fully furnished home."

She and her client agreed to meet at her office and they departed. Before she left, she gave Wilson a very quizzical stare followed by a big smile.

Wilson called a number. When a party answered, he said, "This is Michael. I need you to buy me a house. The realtor is Steve Richards, Richards Realty, and he will be expecting you within the hour. I promised him an extra $5,000 cash bonus after the deal. I need alarm hardware and I need someone to dress a wound. No, I am fine. I'll be at the house you're buying."

With that, he closed the phone and walked inside. In the garage, Wilson smashed the phone on the floor and picked up the pieces to drop into a nearby trashcan. *Well, nothing better to do right now than walk around and check out my new house,* he thought.

His "quick" bag was nearly the size of his Marine Corps duffle bag and it contained his life right now: some cash, his clothes, freeze dried food, a couple more disposable phones, some intricate small tools, weapons and enough ammunition to make a 200-lb man wince just picking it up. Michael Wilson was just that. He stood 6'-2", 220-lbs. At age 32, Wilson was really a machine when he focused on something or someone.

Most of his time in the Corps was spent in a little-known CIA sanctioned unit that awarded him a dark green shoulder patch with a small skull and crossbones that even most officers had no understanding of. He had that patch sewn on his bag when he got out. Spending time in Operation Phoenix had changed him. For one thing, he became more deadly; for another he loathed politics. He chose to focus on the job and not the "why's". This was the reason he was handpicked for the job he held now by the most powerful man in the world.

A half-hour had passed when there was a knock on the front door. Standing already to the side with the familiar .45 in his hand, Wilson looked out. He studied the attractive woman in the business suit holding a large briefcase before opening the door.

"Yes?" he asked.

"Hi, my name is Cathy Robinson and I understand someone at this address requested the services of a healthcare specialist?"

"Are you selling?" Wilson asked.

"No, treating."

He opened the door and invited her in. It was always impressive how fast the folks supporting him responded. She was quite pretty; and she was not wearing any rings. She moved quickly through the small house finding the bedroom. The window shade was down. Turning on the light, she opened the briefcase on the dresser and lifted out a small 9-mm automatic as Wilson took careful aim cocking the hammer back on his .45.

Without flinching, she laid her gun on the dresser and pulled out a packaged metal tray. She unwrapped it and did the same with several instruments, syringes, and a suture package from her briefcase. To this, she added a handful of Betadine-treated sponges. As she removed her glasses and her suit jacket, she turned to Wilson. She looked to be about his age and had a Playboy model's body if those tight clothes spoke the truth.

"I work much better without a .45 trained on me. I also suggest you stop undressing me with your eyes and get yourself undressed. Let me have a look at what I need to attend to."

Wilson asked, "What's your name?"

"Look, I doubt we will even see each other again. Besides, I told you my name."

Wilson asked again, "What's your real name?"

She placed her hands on her hips and gave him a frosty look. Clearly, she was not going to win this contest and her orders were to do anything he asked. After a few more seconds, she said, "My name is Rita".

He met her glare and said, "Mine's Mike. Alright, I'll let you treat me. No drugs, no shots, just do what you need to do."

When Wilson began to remove his shirts, he found the tee shirt was stuck to his skin. The dried blood coagulated like glue. She stepped over and asked if he was hurt anywhere else. He shook his head no.

She told him to go stand in the bathtub without his clothes as she looked into her briefcase. Wilson left the room and with some pain, removed his shoes, socks, pants, before stepping into the tub. He could not get the shirt off without tearing open the wound even more so he waited. His right hand still held the .45.

Rita walked into the bathroom with clean underwear and a pint bottle labeled "saline". There he was standing in a bathtub wearing his tee shirt and underwear. He thought he detected a smirk. She shook her head slightly and said, "You are definitely a Kodak moment". She poured the cool liquid over his tee shirt soaking it and across the wound while gently pulling the shirt away. It began to bleed.

She wetted a Betadine sponge.

"Use this. After you put on your clean underwear, hold this sponge against your wound and come see me. No shirt."

He did so and came back, wobbly. He was getting ready to pass out. She gestured to the bed and told him to lay on his right side. Wilson walked around the bed so he would be facing her and lay down, switching the .45 to his left hand. He felt weak. He was shutting down. A little worry began setting in. What was in that bottle?

"Unless you think you are going to be using that gun anytime soon, maybe you could find a place for it?" she asked.

She removed her shoes, picked up the medical tray and walked to his side of the bed. Wilson didn't care. He had passed out.

Rita went to work. She was at her best when she was most comfortable. Other than being angry and the tissue torn, some of the wound was mostly superficial and cleaned up really well. She sealed it with a wet pack so he could shower. Upon a closer examination, the rest of his body showed no other wounds. In fact, the rest of his body looked rather good. She made it a point to look him over. Thoroughly, actually. She smiled and gave him a small shot of morphine before covering him with a thin blanket.

In the bathroom, Rita picked up his shirt, underwear, pants, socks, and shoes. She rinsed the tub before coming back with his clothes to the bedroom.

There was an old rocker in the corner, which looked inviting. She sat down to protect him. It was somewhat peaceful and his muscled body was easy to look at. She rocked quietly for hours. As the sun began to set, she heard movement outside the front yard. It was followed by a knock on the door. She put the 9mm automatic in her waistband and picked up his .45, moving quickly to the front of the tiny house.

Her orders were no one in. She looked out a side curtain. The person at the door was a female and knocked again.

Rita opened the door and holding the .45 behind her leg, gave a big smile. "Hi, can I help you?"

Denise Harrington was confused and showed it. "Is Michael Wilson here? I brought his papers and the keys to his house. His representative signed everything."

"Oh, hi, I'm Cathy Robinson, his girlfriend." They shook hands. "I made Michael take a nap. He was up all night and we plan to celebrate. I am afraid he was sleepier than he thought. You know men. Big babies."

Denise rolled her eyes and laughed. "I didn't realize Mr. Wilson had a girlfriend, especially one so pretty. I am Denise Harrington, the listing realtor, and my grandmother used to own this house. I was hoping to show him a few of its quirks, but I can do that another time. Here are the papers, keys, and my card. Please have him call me if he wants me to show him anything. Anything at all."

"That's so sweet of you Denise. Thank you for the compliment. Mike will be so grateful you brought the keys and papers over. I will be sure to tell him that you are willing to spend some time with him. Thank you again." She closed the door.

Rita watched Denise get into her car and drive away. Oh brother, she thought. Denise was pretty too, but she definitely was disappointed to find another woman here. She clicked her tongue and laughed softly. Well, at least she had good taste. Whoever this guy was, he was a looker.

Rita stopped in the bedroom doorway when she saw the bed was empty. She took a deep breath, backed up, and went into a crouched position. She had heard nothing. Could Denise have been a diversion?

A man's voice said, "I'm right behind you."

Rita whirled and came up with both guns, one in each hand, both pointed at his head. Standing only in his underwear, Wilson had both palms raised. For the first time he exhibited a bit of a smile.

"Hey doc, you're pretty good."

She slipped the safety into the ON position on his .45 and handed it back to him, butt first. Without saying a word, she walked back into the bedroom with her automatic and packed up her briefcase. She picked up everything in sight she had brought and pushed the eyeglasses onto her face.

She dropped the 9mm gun into her briefcase, snapped the latches and walked out of the bedroom. Mike had not moved. His half-smile was still there.

"Look, Rita, I'm sorry for sneaking up on you. Thanks for fixing me up."

"First, you didn't sneak up on me. I knew where you were; I just did not know if anyone else had gotten in while I was getting the house keys from your over-friendly realtor, Denise. By the way, she gave me her card and said you could call her for anything. I think the emphasis was on "anything". The keys and your papers are on the front table with her card." She half-laughed, but she could feel some jealousy. Jeeze, she hoped it wasn't showing. Why did she care?

"Rita, had you not given me something I wouldn't have been knocked out."

"Look. I never gave you anything. You were fatigued, up all night, flooded with adrenalin I suspect, and your body at some point began to shut down. You willingly gave in probably knowing you were safe. And you were safe you know. I was told to protect you until you were back on your feet."

Wilson thought about this for a second before asking, "So, had I needed you to stay for a few days, you would have?"

"Yes, but you obviously don't need me for that now. Take it slow and don't aggravate that dressing for five or six days."

"Next time, I'll make sure not to recover so fast."

Rita turned and walked to the front door. She stopped long enough to say, "Let's hope there is not a next time for this," and walked out the door.

Wilson noted a large box on the front steps. The corner of it had the name TIMBER. The company was his. The alarm equipment had arrived. He brought it in, opened the box and found some tools. Under the hardware were clean clothes and a cash bundle. He needed it all. Well, nothing like the present to get started. He would be awake all night anyway.

The sun came back up before Wilson had finished and had the alarm's sensitivity set to his liking. He opened his quick bag and spent the next two hours cleaning weapons. Once they were oiled and wrapped, he felt better. None of his guns had ever failed him. He was a strong believer in taking care of his guns so they took care of him. Now that was out of the way, he needed an escape plan. There was no time to dig another tunnel.

He walked around the exterior and decided which entry they might try for and the best place for back-up teams. He did this repeatedly until he was satisfied. He set the perimeter alarm and lay down on the bed for a short nap with his .45 cocked and ready to go. He thought back to when he first met Maria Styletti.

Maria showed up on a sunny spring day in Washington D. C. with a van full of her worldly possessions from the state of Oregon. He was sitting on his rear deck sipping a cold beer, feet up, thinking how nice it was to be back from Asia. He heard a dragging noise on his front porch and grabbed his .45 only to open the door to find this blonde vivacious college graduate moving in next door. She was very cute, wearing a halter-top that was working hard to hold in what was obviously fighting to get out as she stood up. She probably stood about 5'-3", and he guessed her weight to be about 115 pounds. She had a gorgeous tan.

"Oh God!" she said when she saw the gun at his side. She dropped the end of the overstuffed chair and put both hands up to her cheeks.

"Sorry, habit. I work in enforcement, federal." He gave her his best smile.

"Could you put it away? I'm deathly scared of guns."

"Yes, yes, right now," and he did.

They started over and shook hands. He helped her get moved in, took her shopping for those move-in extras one first needs, and then finished the evening off with pizza at Potenza's near the White House. She was excited to be in D.C. They were both surprised to find themselves exiting the next morning at sunrise to jog.

While running, she shared she had been hired at the National Archives and her family was concerned she might end up being a victim of someone or something, living alone in D.C. It was then he told her not to worry. Over the weeks and months after work, they often ate together and went for walks. On occasion when her mom would call, she would insist on speaking with Wilson. She wanted to make sure he was taking good care of her Maria. It was sometime then they moved beyond being strangers. He told her he could not be "that guy" though. She said she was married to her work so it did not matter anyway. They both laughed at that. They knew they were getting closer each day. Maria had a great sense of humor. She was full of spirit and her view of the world was so innocent. Sex with Maria was soft and gentle; he cherished it more than he let on.

Thinking back, this caused Wilson even more angst. He needed to start at the beginning. They had come after him fast and hard. Not many things today warrant such a final response. What had she stumbled across? He closed his eyes and replayed the last 30-some hours in his mind.

3. DEATH OF A FRIEND

Jeff Tompkins was a friend. They had met in Quantico when Wilson had returned for additional tactical training. They had many things in common, but most of all they both enjoyed laughter and drinking beer. He was a new feebie back then. Later, Wilson followed his career with the F.B.I. whenever he was stateside. He had been promoted and was currently one of the Special Agents in Charge – SAC - for the D.C. area. He had not seen Jeff in years when one night he called Wilson's cell phone to suggest they get a beer. Wilson had just landed from the Middle East from taking out a man named Rynard Speer. Speer held many citizenships including American.

A cold beer sounded great. He was curious how Jeff got this cell number too, but then again it was a government issued phone. Jeff offered to pick him up at Reagan Airport. Wilson told him to make it the Air Force base, Joint Base Andrews, formerly known to most folks as Andrews Air Force Base. Jeff paused and said he would head that way.

Being an FBI agent can get you onto most American bases around the world; being a SAC FBI agent gets you in faster, especially if your office calls ahead. Someone had to have done just that. Jeff was standing by his sedan at the doors to the 11th Wing when Wilson walked outside. The night air was warm and he was glad to be back in America. They shook hands and Wilson asked to put his bag in the trunk of his car. Jeff popped the trunk and Wilson set his bag inside. He removed his .45 from it and placed the gun into the small of his back. Jeff raised his eyebrows, but said nothing.

"So, what's the FBI want with me that they would ask my friend to buy me a beer to find out," I asked, climbing into his car.

He shut his door and started the engine. "Who said I was buying," he laughed.

He told me I looked pretty good except for needing a shave. I told him for a "suit" he looked boring. We both laughed. I noted Jeff went out of his way to drive to the Yellow Dog Tavern in Baltimore, passing several pubs along the way. He kept the conversation going, but we both knew this was a longer ride than necessary just for beer. We pulled up and parked.

"Are we meeting someone here?" I asked, "Or did you just want to get me alone for that big boy hug?" I laughed again. It was good to see Jeff and I had no role in any local action so my thoughts were clear.

We went inside with me following Jeff to a corner unto itself.

"Wow, we really are on a date, aren't we," I quipped.

The waitress came and we ordered a pitcher of Bud Light.

"How well do you know your neighbor, Maria?" Jeff tossed out.

"What's Maria done to warrant the Bureau's interest, besides looking 'hot?" I asked.

"Did I say she had done anything?"

"It's what you didn't say. You did not bring me all the way out here to find out if I would set you up on a date. See? This is why people do not like the FBI. You tease them into thinking they are the only one, ply them with alcohol, and then want to cheat on them with their neighbor."

Jeff locked his eyes on mine and said, "You can save me a lot of time if I know what you know of her and how close the two of you were. It's classified, Mike."

"Well, you're a SAC, you can de-classify it if you want my answer or wait until I read it for myself when I get into work tomorrow."

"Speaking of that, where exactly does Michael Wilson work? You have never said. I know you have some juice if you will slip a .45 into your belt in front of an FBI agent, in D.C. of all places. The fact that you use flights out of Andrews is telling."

We drank in silence before Jeff said, "Please."

"See, that's all it took. We're friends." I smiled, "Maria is really a nice person. I enjoy her company and her laughter, and she has a good heart. I helped her move some furniture into her condominium about seven, maybe eight months ago. That's how we met. As you said, she is my neighbor. She came from somewhere in Oregon. Her family is very close and her mom especially was very concerned about a single girl moving to Washington D.C. I elected myself her designated "protector". We hit it off. We have dinner sometimes. We even jog together on occasion. Sometimes we have a sleep over. She has a key to my condo and brings the mail in for me since I'm on the road a lot. That's it my friend."

"Do you know where Maria works and what she does?" he asked.

"Well, she supervises or chairs a 9/11materials committee that files or catalogs the information from the commission and

19

other sources as it comes in. She works over at the National Archives. It's historical stuff. I know she enjoys her work, but we have an understanding not to talk about work since both of us have confidential agreements."

"Maria Styletti went missing two days ago, right before a secret House sub-committee grilled CIA people from the Psychological Warfare Department on, of all things, 9/11," Jeff said.

He was taking a chance admittedly. I was her neighbor. He knew I worked in government, but he was not sure where. My files held a classification of 'Top Secret – Clearance V' only. Unless you had the consensus of two other Agency Directors and were a Director yourself, you were not getting a peek into my life. Only a sitting President had singular authority. I was sure Jeff tried to get access and failed before telling his folks he would talk to me on his own.

He continued on, "Here is where I entered the picture. One of the federal judges on that panel, Cheryl Henderson is a close friend. She asked me discreetly to see what I could find out. Apparently, Maria and she struck up a friendship since both are conspiracy fans – my words, not Cheryl's. Maria called her at home the night before she disappeared. Cheryl was out and Maria sounded frantic, said she would try someone else. When I found out who her neighbor was, I was thinking maybe she tried you. Others might too. Here is the kicker. Styletti said she came across a file that she was sure no one had made public. It suggested the government played a role in 9/11 if I understood the Judge correctly. Just saying that could put anyone at risk with some of the people in this town. There are still some here that feel a need to protect secrets at any cost. These things can take on a life of their own. She has definitely vanished, Mike."

Maria missing was a concern to me too. I had to set emotions aside, but the truth was, I really liked her. I sat there and took all this in. There had to have been something she stumbled across while filing papers or looking at files in the Archives. There were many secrets there, several I knew worth killing for. The chances of her being abducted by a stranger I thought were almost nil. Whoever it was, I would find them.

"Look, Jeff. It's late, I'm tired and this is a lot for me to take in. Why don't you give me time tomorrow to see what I can find out? I have other sources as well. Maybe I can call Maria's mom and see if Maria had spoken to her. We can meet back here tomorrow night for a flat iron steak and some of their pommes fries. I will even buy dinner. Say 7 PM?"

"Well, if you're buying dinner, how can I turn that down? All right, we'll meet here at 7 PM. Thanks. If you turn up something and need a hand with it, call me, here is my personal card. Oh, and Mike, be careful until we know what is really going on. Some of these people ..." His voice trailed off and he waved a hand in the air.

I never had just one home. I pretended I did. I used my condo for that. He dropped me off there. I went inside and found it looked good, too good. Someone had taken it apart and put it back together. Magazines were stacked neater than I had left them. Some of the furniture had been moved and not quite put back in their original rug indentations. My pillows were fluffed and the open ends placed the opposite of how I had left them.

It had been a while since I had been home. I was not that neat. There were no phone messages. Maria would have left a message if she'd called me. I knew it. She did not know where I worked, but when she saw my .45 while she was moving in, I had let her think I was some sort of federal cop. I was counting on the fact that whoever did the search would not think to look for hidden video. I checked my mini-computer on the wall shelf behind my painting of the Capitol. The hard drive had been formatted. It was wiped clean. Someone brought a professional tech with them. Now, I had no surveillance of who they were. I checked the separate room audio hidden in my living room wall electrical outlet. It was my back-up. One might say I was paranoid. I liked to think of myself as careful. I took the chip out, put it in my iPhone, and hit play. Bingo. It was soft, but I could hear her voice. Someone had played back Maria's phone call to me.

"Mike, this is Maria. I need help. I'm scared. I found something in a file I don't think anyone has ever seen. It is really, really disturbing. Call me as soon as you get this, please Mike. Please."

My throat tightened when I heard her plea. Someone had come into my home; that same someone probably had Maria. It was time to hunt the hunters.

I entered her apartment from her balcony, carrying my quick bag. Her place was ransacked. The bedroom showed signs of a struggle. They must have waited until she was asleep to grab her.

For me, there could be no sleeping now. I grabbed my bag and jumped into my truck. I called Jeff and left a message on his direct line, that I had contact from Maria and he was on the right path. Call my cell.

I showed my I.D. and drove through the heavily guarded gates at the building where I had been given an office only a year ago. The night staff was there and they were surprised to see me. I waved them off, went into my office, and closed the door. I started making electronic inquiries about Maria.

There was a lot more to Maria Styletti than I had known.

I read that she was the executive administrator for the sub-committee that Agent Tompkins had referenced. Her listed duties said she was charged with cataloging and supervising the filing of all photos and written materials related to 9/11 that were being held by all agencies or other sources so they might be placed in one central repository: the National Archives. She had been continuously pushing for the release of all CIA records. Something must have piqued her interest to point her in that direction. Persistence into the shadows of D.C. was usually met with unpleasantness.

I pushed myself back from the computer and thought about conversations we had, had. Then it came to me. I remember Maria saying if I ever read her Sally Sue computer, I would really think she was paranoid. She kept an electronic diary on a separate computer somewhere. She had named it Sally Sue making it easier to talk to it. We both laughed. If it was connected to the Internet, I could locate it and access it, no matter where in the world it was.

I logged into a restricted venue and set my computer search on "Sally Sue". It was time for some coffee. When I came back, the NSA mainframes at Fort Meade had done their work. "Sally Sue" produced many results, but the one I wanted and the one I began reading was from a computer that NSA remotely logged into. It was all Maria.

Maria had typed several notes about some of the people she worked with, their cooperation or lack of cooperation. She noted that most agencies cooperated with her requests except the CIA's Psychological Warfare Department.

The last entry was dated the day she disappeared. She had scanned a file of notes she placed inside her daily filings. It was not an accident. It was from an anonymous informant. Her receiving and handling this file would warrant a federal death sentence. Clearly, this is what caused her to be so afraid. This file was an analysis of 9/11 complete with unseen photos. It was marked "Presidential Eyes Only." This had to have come from a vault.

Many Americans including myself had many questions about the Twin Towers collapsing into dust. Many, again including me, wondered why the videos on the exterior of the Pentagon and from area traffic cams as well as business cams had been seized and never released. There was never a plane found there. There were never any contact points from the wings – just a hole.

The French government said it was from a missile but never explained those first comments. Israel concurred.

I looked at the Pentagon analysis first. The FBI seized 84 videos for it and the CIA immediately took possession of them before they were viewed. The most revealing one came from a Sheraton National Hotel recording that clearly showed a cruise missile coming in low hitting the Pentagon.

My computer flashed that someone was trying to capture my login. I had about seven seconds. I quickly went through and read another memo about a guy named Alejandro Rodriguez. He was the only person with a master key to the North Tower stairwell. He was in the basement, under ground level when he heard first one, then a second explosion. This was seven to eight minutes *before* the first plane hit. As he mounted the underground stairwells, he noted explosive packets in every corner. He rescued fifteen people and was the last man out before it disappeared into dust.

Flash: three-seconds left. I had to exit.

I inserted our emergency USB drive and hit enter. The drive destroyed all my history and replaced it with a false log just before "Compromised" flashed on screen. The USB finished by formatting the drive. Someone was tracking Maria, "Sally Sue," , me, or all of us.

Maria must have called Judge Henderson for guidance when she first received this without telling her what it was.

Computers are great, but you always leave a footprint when you walk through someone else's backyard. I marveled at our IT being prepared for this inevitability and left the building. There was a lot to think about.

My "time" using the NSA mainframes at Fort Meade would be logged to my boss. He might want to know what I was searching for since I was on "leave" and why it was necessary to conceal my search results.

On the drive home it came over my truck radio that a fatality accident had closed the Arlington Bridge. I re-routed around the Potomac to get home. I was hungry and stopped in at a remodeled Wendy's to get a spicy chicken sandwich. The staff seemed in a really good mood that I attributed not only to their camaraderie but the fact that this Wendy's was spotless and state-of-the-art. Rather then most of the seating being single hard chairs, booths had been returned and the eating was more inviting. Breaking news was on their flat screen TV's as I sat down to eat. The anchor reported that FBI Agent Tompkins assigned to the D.C. area had just died on the Arlington Bridge in a fiery car crash. Details were scarce but the anchor said they would have more as the investigation unfolded. It appeared a tire had blown out sending the driver into the path of a large truck.

Based on my experience, I did not believe in coincidences. This was no accident. Somebody had followed Jeff, which meant they probably had seen me. It was time to vanish. I mentally tucked what I believed was Jeff's real fate away. I took an extra five minutes to drive down the Cascades Parkway and toss my cell phone onto the nearest boat moored on the Potomac.

When I arrived in my neighborhood, I noted two teams, one at each end of the block closing in where I lived. I got out of my truck, grabbed my quick bag, walked into my place, out the sliding door, over the balcony to the ground, and took off running.

I took the subway and jogged to the house I had bought a couple years ago. It's where they triggered the silent vibrating alarm that set me on the run. It was a great house and I had it wired the way I preferred. Digging a tunnel was just a back-up plan. I had really thought I would have that home for a long time. It angered me that they forced me to leave it. Someone was going to compensate me for that.

No bodies were there and my place had been cleaned up except for the broken glass I had shot out. My determination grew even fiercer. It was time to get back to my new house. I headed out.

I proceeded cautiously to insure I was not followed.

A cursory check revealed my new house was still secure and I went inside. I double-checked all windows and doors before re-setting the alarm.

I needed some rest and closed my eyes this time hoping to sleep.

4. READY TO GO

I awoke refreshed and found the sun had gone back down. It was dark. I got up and pulled down all the window shades. I turned on only the necessary lights. I purposely lit up the living room brighter than the others and turned on the TV. If they were going to hit, I wanted them to hit there first. It would give me more time.

Shaving and showering brought back thoughts of my being shot. I should have taken a moment to focus and think before I kept going last night. I had been sloppy opening the car door. Finding this house had been good but I knew it was temporary while I got help. A flood of thoughts entered my mind and I felt it best to think while I toweled off. They would be more cautious next time. Their net outside would be wider and reinforced. They would expect that would end this.

He dressed quickly. He was hungry so he armed up. He slipped the .45 into the small of his back and the compact 9mm into his pocket pulling his over-sized tee shirt down to cover both of them. It was time to see if his "new" car started. He placed the quick bag in the trunk. He re-set the alarm, pressed the Chamberlain button on the wall and crouched down while the door opened. He climbed into the car and started it up. While eyeing all his surroundings, he slowly backed out and pressed the garage door opener on the key chain to close the garage. He had a quarter-tank of gas.

He drove south on the freeway for no reason other than looking for gas. Off the third exit was a Keg Steakhouse. It sounded good. He pulled into a Chevron across from it and pumped regular into the tank. Since they could track a credit card within hours, he paid cash. He looked around before getting back in the car, and drove across the street into the Keg parking lot. It was only half-full but he parked near the back anyway.

The hostess offered to seat him in the bar, but a drink would dull his senses. He opted for a booth facing the front doors and sat down. His waiter, Jon, wanted to chat, but he cut him off with a steak order saying he had an appointment and his tip would be dependent if he left here on time.

The first bite of that 12-ounce charcoal broiled steak made him salivate. It was perfect. It made him realize he had not eaten in over 24-hours. He stared at the grill marks, the light crust of seasoning on it, and the medium-pink inside. The baked potato was crisp on the outside just as he enjoyed them. With butter, sour cream, cheese, and bacon on it, it looked like desert. All of it went down fast. The asparagus tips were crunchy and delicious. Butter oil on the plate, bits of charcoal from the steak and brown bread to soak it all up finished it off. A little fat never hurt anyone he thought. He was out of there in less than a half-hour and left a good tip for Jon.

Again, Wilson looked around and unlocked the Ford. He began to climb in and froze. On the seat was a folded piece of paper. Wilson crouched quickly pulling out the .45, thumbing the safety off. "What the hell?" he thought. He moved quickly to the treed area of the lot because that is where they had to be. He came up empty handed. Wilson retrieved the note and abandoned his "new" car. He watched as an old couple arrived in a newer Impala.

Someone had printed "Do not go back to the house. They know."

Well, if "they" had placed the note, they simply would have killed him when he came out of The Keg. So, who was his new friend? More importantly, where was he going to stay now? Had someone followed him to the restaurant? Were they watching him now? And, if they were watching him, was someone watching *them*?

He didn't need to wipe off his fingerprints. He didn't have any. They had been obliterated when he was younger. He decided to abandon the Ford since it had been associated with him and ran. He was trained to survive. He had done this before. With the .45 in one hand and the quick bag in the other, he ran uphill, through the cloudy night, across farm fields, zigzagging for what seemed like miles through heavy crops until he could run no more. He knew he had for well over 3 or even 4-hours. Then, that was a weekly workout for him – just not uphill through heavy brush. His gunshot abrasion burned from the salt in his sweat. He stopped and sat down under a tree on a hillside. The houses and their lights below were barely dots. Maybe they were stars. He needed to get his wind. He needed water. Eating that baked potato might not have been such a good idea after all. These guys were better at information gathering than he thought.

Wilson's friend, Robbie, had followed his progress through a hand night scope after placing the note inside the car. There wasn't anything more he could do without bringing attention to himself. Robbie, who worked at the NSA, had seen the chatter about a rogue agent. Against all rules, he focused his own computer on that subject for a few seconds, only to learn the rogue agent was his friend. He owed Mike and Robbie believed this would make them even. He knew Wilson would never go rouge. He decided to leave his car and take Mike's back to the house. Opening Mike's Ford's car door, he started it with a pocket screwdriver and drove back to North Glen to help alter Wilson's path. The neighborhood looked quiet. If "they" were anywhere, they would be inside the garage. He had gotten there before them and quickly wired a very small pack of C4 inside it. He later caught up with Mike exiting the freeway by pure luck and decided to alter his plan a little. He would try to find out more by going back to the house.

The whole afternoon had been one lucky event after the other starting with seeing an "eyes only" from Defense Intel stating Michael Wilson had recently purchased a house. The CIA had quietly requested his known location from all agencies. Robbie had allowed questionable things to happen over the years as a government employee, but his role in this one would be a surprise to many if they ever learned of it. He recognized the danger. He owed Mike his life and maybe this would allow him time to get away.

When he saw Mike in the Ford he knew what he had to do.

Now, it was show time. He pressed the garage door opener and as the door opened, he could picture them getting ready. He thought, "We're even Mike". He pressed the remote quickly three times. By the time the garage blew up he had already backed up into the neighbor's yard. Quietly, he opened the driver's door to engage any that came out from around the house. While he was a combat-tested Marine, he was not trained for this. He never really had a chance. She shot him in the head as he sensed her presence. It came too quickly.

She walked over and kneeled down. Shit. It was not Michael Wilson.

5. MAKING A NEW ALLY

Wilson woke up to the sun's first rays and one of the largest wolf-like German Shepherd dogs he had ever seen. There was an old man about his build with a shotgun standing beside him silently. The old man coughed into a handkerchief.

"I have to believe there must be something redeeming about you or this animal would have torn you apart, .45 or no .45," he said with one boot on Wilson's gun.

The shotgun was not pointed at him, but he held it like a man that had skillfully used one before and could again in an instant. Still, Wilson might have tried to disarm him, but it was not going to happen with that wolf present.

"I apologize for being on your property," Wilson said. "I fell asleep without intending to. May I get up?"

"You know son, you've been sizing me up since your eyes left this animal. You should be keeping your eyes on him. Instead, my guess is you were probably thinking about trying to take my shotgun even before I saw you thinking it. However, that's not going to happen, not today, not with Prince standing here."

When he said Prince, the animal didn't move, didn't growl, just flashed his teeth. It got my attention. They were big. Hell, he was big.

"Alright, I guess we are kind of at a standstill here. Neither one of us wants to harm the other I hope. I'd be happy if you let me stand up and walk off your property," I said.

He looked at Prince, took his boot off my .45 and picked it up. He put it inside my quick bag and hoisted it. The old man was strong because that bag weighed over 45 pounds and he never flinched. He walked away. I stood up, but was quickly pushed to the ground by two large paws and another flash of teeth. This time there was a growl. The old man never looked back, but he did muffle a laugh. He quietly called for Prince to follow.

This time I stood up slowly. Prince never moved. I cautiously began walking after the old man and Prince followed me.

We walked in silence for about two hours or more before he pointed out his farmhouse. I still did not see it. We were almost at the front door before I made it out. It was down in a depression between two rolling hills of corn. Its roof was hidden, as were most of its wood and brick sides. It really looked more like a big hill the more I thought about it. Clever.

At the door, the old man stopped and made a circle motion to Prince. The dog took off at a run leaving us. The old man opened the door.

"Come inside. You'll be safe unless Prince tells me different. He is doing a perimeter check. The nice thing about him is he is fast, quiet, and deadly if need be. It's kind of like having my own Indian scout. He found you."

I looked behind and the dog was gone. I could not leave without hurting the old man to get my bag and he had been kind to me. I wasn't going to do that. Besides, my wound hurt like hell.

"You're free to go after Prince gets back if you feel the need. Not before. He knows you don't have permission," the old man said "And don't think having a gun will make a difference. It doesn't to him. He's kind of like a ghost. Here, there, gone. Then, back again."

I walked over to the small kitchen and turned the cold water on. I cupped my hands and drank until my thirst was gone and wiped my hands on my jeans.

He waited until I was done, shrugged his shoulders, and said, "You can continue to drink and eat with your hands or you can help yourself to my ware in the cupboards." I noted he had not put the shotgun away yet and he caught me eyeing it.

"This shotgun is not for you. Until Prince tells me it's safe outside, the shotgun always stays in my hands. And, yup, it's always loaded. No point in having a gun if it's empty."

Awkward. None of this was threatening, but I didn't like it. I had no control and I could not leave. At least he thought so.

"Look. There are some pretty bad people out there and I have no idea if they are behind me. You should give me my stuff back and call your animal in," I stated.

"Well, that's just not going to happen young man. Prince has his own thoughts about finishing something when he is told to do it. When he gets back, we'll make a decision about you next," he said, dropping my bag at my feet.

He walked over to his refrigerator, set the shotgun against the side of it and pulled out a couple eggs and some bacon. Without another word, he commenced to cooking breakfast. He set up two plates, took control of the shotgun, and we sat down to eat. None of this seemed extraordinary to him. It still was to me.

About the time he was removing the plates and pouring coffee, Prince appeared panting in the doorway. The old man asked if the property was clear and Prince laid down where he stood. I guessed that meant "yes". The old man thanked him and set out a bowl of dog food with some bacon grease on it along with a large bowl of fresh water. Prince drank and ate in silence.

This was some act they had, but I had to move on before I brought trouble to this old man and his wonder dog.

"My name's Gus," said the old man. He sat down at the table and extended his hand.

"I'm Mike. Mike Wilson." We shook hands. "Look Gus, you seem like a nice guy and I don't want to bring my trouble here. I should go." I stood up to leave. Prince didn't even turn his head in my direction.

"Well, you look like a smart fella and in need of a place to stay. I have more food than you can eat. No one knows this farmhouse is here. You're safe. It doesn't show up on the county records. Prince here would welcome your company. Besides, that blood on your shirt tells me you need a friend. Please, wait here. I need to check on something and get some bandages. I'll be back. Please, wait."

I looked down and pulled my shirt out from my side. My bandage had not been happy with my physical activity the last 24-hours.

Gus was back in about 20 minutes. There was a satisfactory look on his face. He was more relaxed. He set down a rather worn leather medical bag.

"Come here a minute," he said.

36

He walked me around the outside of the house. Gus pointed out a few "trap" areas he said to avoid should I walk outside without him. We went back inside. He took me down a short hallway that led to a large bathroom and two bedrooms. The larger one was obviously his. The other was empty except a bed, small dresser and an old TV. I was guessing it was for company, which by the looks of it had never seen.

Gus brought out a shot glass and a bottle of Jack Daniels. He handed me a flannel Pendleton shirt from his closet and said, "Pour yourself a couple of quick shots then take off your shirt and I'll clean that wound. I have a little experience in that area."

The Jack Daniels burned my throat. Gus took the bottle and shot glass back to the kitchen. He scrubbed his hands and returned to stand in front of me.

I peeled off the bandage. I looked at him in a different light. There was something about his moves, how he acted in the moment, and his knowledge. Clearly, there was more to Gus than I had given him credit for. He cleaned my wound as if he had done it before. When he removed the dual-syringe that held the gel-liquid bandage, I knew he held allegiance to someone or something. An American company invented it for military wounds. It was designed not to stick to the wound, just the skin. It was good at resisting abrasions as well. Moreover, it had not been released to civilian physicians yet.

"Do you know what this is," Gus asked. "This is the dandiest stuff. It is kind of a miracle liquid bandage. When the press learned about it in Iraq they called it the spray-on bandage. It is pain free, doesn't stick to anything but the skin, and with your wound, you'll heal up in a week I suspect."

Our eyes locked and Gus gave me a knowing nod. Clearly, we set our suspicions aside based on some sort of unspoken trust. He applied it and I waited to speak until he had finished and closed his bag.

"Well, if you cook like you treat your patients, I'd like to stay a couple days and rest up as you say. Thanks Gus." We shook hands again and the smile on his face said I had made the right decision.

"Mike, you know where your room is. Take your bag and set it in the closet. I usually go for a walk after breakfast and see what's new on the farm. If you're up to it, we can do it together."

I did just that. There was something about the old man and this animal that I liked. I must have been getting soft. Well, not too soft. I brought the .45.

He pointed out a fake, but very real looking, two-man rock near the front door. It hid access to a 200' garbage shaft. What wasn't eaten was dropped into it; everything else was burned in the sealed fireplace. We started walking. We could have walked in circles for all I knew. Everything looked the same and yet, everything looked different. Gus seemed to think we were getting somewhere so I really didn't pay attention to more than the unexpected. I let him talk, but I had no idea why he was telling me this. He didn't appear one to ramble on without a purpose.

He praised the land and its crops saying he had been a good steward of the property. He had owned it for many years before he retired, but had only lived on it for the past ten years or so.

It was a challenge to balance crop cutting and maintaining the overall aspects of seclusion. Some of the plantings were artificial. Some were disbursed among real plants too.

The house was built to his design and it cost almost as much to hide it as it did to build it he said. He didn't want anyone to be able to drive to it, walk to it, or even see it from the air. It was not vulnerable to heat-seeking nor any other disclosure he was aware of. While he owned a little over 3,000 acres, his property butted National Forest on one side and one of the largest private ranches in Virginia on the other. It was only natural to assume this land belonged to one or the other – or both. Some crops were deliberate and brush grew wild. Both had strategic placement. It was what he wanted.

Gus explained that for him retirement meant solitude. And solitude meant security. We walked a little more and I could see an old well with a pump house. Gus opened the door and pointed to a hand pump from which he pumped some cold water into a tin cup for both of us. With some effort he then rotated it 180 degrees.

There was a whoosh and I could hear hydraulics as a large area of corn stalks moved down into the ground, out of sight, and a Jeep sitting on a paved pad came back up in its place.

Gus winked at me and said, "One can build anything if one has enough money. Are you doing okay? Do we need to get back, Mike?"

I had seen a lot of things in my short life. Most of the impressive ones that I had seen, had been owned or made by the government. Secret, of course. This one was pretty slick.

"No, I feel okay and my bandage seems to be holding thanks to you."

"Let's go for a ride, then." He activated some sort of compass/navigational screen in the Jeep.

I jumped in knowing with certainty that there was a lot more to Gus than I knew. There is no such thing as coincidence and the fact that I was here – with Gus – was not one. My flags were back up.

We rode out across his property, down a forest access road where he just happen to have a key to the lock and chain that crossed it. He asked me to unlock it and lock it behind him as he drove the Jeep out. It was then I noticed a small black and blue colored insignia on his windshield. We soon entered a back road and came out into a cow pasture passing a huge barn. Gus waved to a ranch hand and we eventually exited on to the highway. That was interesting.

He drove on for another 45 minutes before driving into a small town and parking in front of a small grocery store.

"C'mon on inside with me and I'll introduce you."

I didn't move.

"Gus, I'm not sure that's a good idea for me to be seen with you."

"Don't worry about this place, Mike. The folks that own the store are retired. I paid for their daughter Penny's operation when they found out she had cancer. I'm also the landlord. You're among friends."

I hopped out and made sure the tee was covering my .45. That movement was not lost on Gus, I could tell. So be it.

Inside we went. There were a couple folks sitting around an old stove. The floor looked worn around it like it was the local gathering place. Course with the summer here, it was not lit. They nodded at Gus and he introduced me to each one. Gus emphasized I was family. I wasn't sure what that meant but it seemed to put everyone at ease.

Gus told me to grab a couple cases of water while he grabbed a 50 pound bag of dog chow and some toiletries. He hoisted that onto a shoulder with one hand faster than I moved my two cases of water. He asked Penny to put it on his tab, made his good-byes, and back into the Jeep we went.

"It must take you the better part of a day to walk in groceries to the house from the Jeep's location," I thought aloud.

"Mmm – not really. It just depends on how much I have and whether I want the exercise or not," Gus said.

We drove down the road to the ranch, onto the property and past the large barn once again. No one seemed to care. Soon we came to the locked chain on the forestland and he produced the key once more. I unlocked it and locked it up after he passed. We move down the road and began driving across what I assumed was his property now.

He had been very careful to keep his house indigenous and keep the Jeep even further away from it. He had a somewhat mysterious route into town. He had chosen the place where he did business carefully. Yes, there was a lot to Gus I did not know – yet.

We stopped in the middle of nowhere. Gus pointed ahead and said the pump house was just up there. He moved the Jeep up, closer. We got out and grabbed the supplies. The keys remained in the Jeep. I offered to take the dog chow but Gus would not hear of it. We moved over to the side of the pump house, set things down, and Gus looked over at me.

"Come on over here and let's see if you remember how to put the Jeep away."

I walked over and attempted to rotate the pump. Nothing happened.

"Put some back into it – push harder," Gus said.

This time I pushed for all I was worth. The pump rotated and things started up. Gus was even stronger than I thought he was. He laughed at my expression.

"I figured if someone came across that shack and got themselves some water, I didn't it want the Jeep to just come up," he said, "You learned the knack pretty quickly."

He drove the Jeep onto the platform when it locked into place. Rotating the pump, he sent it back underground.

I put a box of bottled water on each shoulder while Gus hoisted the dog chow and a plastic bag before we moved out. It kind of reminded me of forced marches years ago in the Corps. "Forced" was the operative word. The sun was not our friend then and it wasn't today. Gus expressed concern about my wound, but I had no pain. Looking at my borrowed shirt, there was no seepage.

I could never have found my way back without my compass. I don't know how Gus did it, but he did. It was none too soon. My shoulders were just beginning to ache and now my wound hurt. The sun was going down. I found myself hungry too.

Gus noted it was suppertime and set about making spaghetti. He passed me a Bud Light and suggested I pull up one of the stools while he cooked.

"You saw a lot of my world today, Mike. In fact, you saw more than anyone ever has. I shared it with you because I want you to share your problem with me. I like you son. I liked you right away. I especially appreciated the way you conducted yourself when Prince and I first met you. You may have been able to kill one of us, but I doubt you would have gotten to both of us. Maybe, maybe not. Nevertheless, you showed us respect. I never kid a kidder. You have government written all over you. I'm just trying to figure out which part."

And, there it was. The elephant was in the room.

"Well," Gus said, "you think about it. We'll eat, play some cards – you do play poker, don't you – and just see where this new friendship takes us."

The appearance of Prince broke the ice. Gus served up two plates, poured a little sauce over the chow he had bought Prince, and all of us began to eat. I had to think about this. I was not entirely on my own, but I could use a second set of eyes.

I raised my beer to Gus and said, "To new friends." We banged bottles and chugged them down. Cold beer was a good thing when the time allowed for it.

Since Gus cooked, I thought it only fair to clean up. He had to show me where a few things were. I did tease him about having all this technology and no dishwasher. Gus told me it was just something he enjoyed.

I had to admit; it gave me a bit of satisfaction and allowed me time to think as well.

We played cards. Gus was better at talking than he was playing poker. Good thing we were using chips. Had we been playing for money, the night would have made me pretty rich. I enjoyed his company and tried to return the favor.

I yawned and we decided it was time to hit the sack. Gus walked over to the door and opened it. He came back and finished his beer. Prince appeared in the doorway and Gus told me he was going to set him on patrol before locking up. I headed down the hall to my room.

I lay down on the bed and thought over the past week. I could hear Gus coughing a few times. I figured I would give my wound another two or three days depending on how it looked tomorrow. I wanted to find out who left the note in my car. They probably saved my life. I peeled off my clothes, climbed between the sheets and fell fast asleep.

I woke to the smell of bacon frying and coffee. I had not allowed myself the luxury of sleeping in in a long time. I went down the hall to the bathroom. Setting on the sink for me was a razor, shaving cream, a toothbrush, toothpaste and a hairbrush in a clear plastic bag. I shaved, showered and dressed. My wound looked great. It was down to about a three-inch scrape maybe about a half-inch wide.

Gus hollered that breakfast was on the table and I walked down the hall. I poured myself some coffee and sat down. I was faced with bacon, scrambled eggs, and hot cornbread.

"Jeeze Gus, you messed your calling," I teased him. "You would have made someone a great wife."

"I'll take that as a compliment," he said with a laugh. "So, I take it the bed was comfortable. Your snoring told me so."

"I snore?" I asked, "Sorry for keeping you awake."

"Oh, you didn't. Prince did. He went back and forth between the rooms I think. We don't usually have company and he wanted to make sure I knew someone was staying the night I suspect."

"Speaking of Prince, where is he? I mean, where does he go all the time?"

Gus changed the subject and pushed the cornbread saying it was one of his specialties. It was too.

I cleaned up and put things away. Gus pulled out some sort of small device from behind a large framed photo of Prince, tapped a button, and studied the photo when it changed screens. He put it back, picked up a book from the floor and sat down to read. I stood in the kitchen for a moment and thought how much I had to come to like Gus in such a short time.

I walked down the hall, grabbed my compact 9mm from my bag and put it in my waistband at the small of my back. I just felt better having at least one gun with me at all times.

There was a smile on Gus's face when I came back. He put his finger in his book to mark the place and said if I wanted to kickback, I could join him. I asked why he was smiling.

"I told you, you were safe here. You don't need to carry a gun around all the time, especially inside."

"How'd you know?"

"I heard your bag slide off the closet floor and just figured that's what you were doing. I was young once. Now, I'm old, but I'm a lot smarter. I have measures in place that allow me a certain amount of time to safely react to any threat."

It was my turn to laugh. Prince appeared at his feet. I didn't know where he'd come from. I knew he wasn't in the room when we started talking. A "ghost" is what Gus had said. I'd do well to remember that.

"Gus, can I have you take a look at my wound? It's not bothering me, but I need to get back to what I was doing before you took me in."

He set his book down and went to get his medical bag. I removed the 9mm and took off my shirt. Gus returned and sat down next to me. He walked his fingers all around the bandage carefully looking for tissue response.

"There is only a slight inflammation which is great. That tells me we are doing the right thing here. Let's leave the liquid bandage in place. It does better when it is ready to come off on its own. I think it is progressing nicely, Mike. I would say give it a couple days. I probably should not have had you carry that water inside. Any discomfort?"

"Ah – the discomfort word" I laughed. "You're sure you're not a country doctor? No, actually it is fine. I was hurting a little when I went to bed last night, but this morning it's great."

Gus turned on FOX and we watched Shepherd Smith tell us about an unusual explosion in a neighborhood about 30 miles to the South of us. There were yellow lettered ATF jackets on folks walking around a house that looked like the one I had just bought. As the camera panned back, there was my '65 Ford on a tow-truck. A spokesperson said it appeared an explosion had been triggered as the car was backing out of the garage. The "feds" had control of the investigation, but did not say why. The driver of the car had died.

As Smith began his Around the World segment, I wondered what this meant. Could the person driving my car have been the friend? Or, had they just wanted the car to stage my death? I needed to find out who the driver was.

"Gus, do you happen to have an internet connection by chance?"

"I do, yes."

"Can I ask you what type of encryption you use?"

He gave me a serious look and said, "KG-250."

Somehow, I had given myself away somewhere in the short time I had met him. That wasn't like me. If he knew there was a chance I would understand an algorithm like KG-250, then he thought that I worked for the NSA. No one I knew outside the National Security Agency Intel had access to the KG245-A, or the newer KG-250 programs. In fact, very few people inside the NSA had heard about the KG-250. I chose to remain silent. Gus was testing me again.

"If you're wondering," Gus went on, "some little things have nibbled at me. There are only a couple people that put together quick bags like yours and only two, alive, that I know of, that have your patch. I had to carry it to be certain. Both are Marines and both work or had worked for the NSA. It was rumored that one was still alive and the other one? She hasn't been seen in many years; I figured the one I have is not her." He smiled when he said it.

"Then there is Prince. Prince would never take to anyone. He trusts people less than I do. When he was indifferent to you, I knew you were somebody I should know. Heck, you were somebody I wanted to know. I figured I would see how things unfolded."

I excused myself to get some air. Perhaps now was not the time to reach out. I needed to know more about Gus. Feeling safe was one thing; being safe was another. I did not like the position I found myself in. He had all the information for the time being and I had none. I came back inside.

Gus stood up, grabbed a couple of cold Bud Lights from the refrigerator and suggested we move outside.

Gus told me one of his heroes was William "Wild Bill" Donovan. Gus had met him in 1958 when he was just out of college.

William Donovan started the Office of Strategic Services and then morphed it, with President Roosevelt's blessing, into the Central Intelligence Agency. The NSA followed in 1949 as those in power began carving out their own niche, he said. Donovan thought the place to be for a young scholar like Gus was the NSA. With Donovan as a reference, Gus landed his dream job. Donovan died from a stroke in 1959 before Gus could share his news he was on the hiring list.

Gus visited his grave once a month at Arlington National Cemetery. He made a silent promise to Wild Bill that he would do everything he could to defend America, no matter what it took or where it took him.

"I would tell Bill what was going on in general terms due to my secrecy oath and all. I knew he would appreciate my limitation. I did fill him in on all the politics though and a few Presidential comments we picked up in the air. It would either have infuriated him or given him a chuckle. I wish I could have seen his face to know."

Gus' dedication was rewarded with a steady rise through the ranks. He beamed and said Wild Bill would have been proud.

"I ran a tight ship. I was firm, but fair – and unlike others, never vindictive. I even received a Presidential citation from Reagan that I thought Bill would envy."

When Gus felt he had more than honored the commitment to Wild Bill, he used some connections and money he had saved to purchase his own piece of America over a period of several years. He wanted to do it without drawing attention to himself so when he walked out, it was like an amicable divorce. Gus would never see the family again – or so he told me.

I brought out two more Bud Lights and saluted Gus with a toast thanking him for being honorable and for his duty to the country. The sun was beginning to set.

"Tell you what Gus. Let me cook tonight. I'll see what you have in the cupboards and try not to poison either one of us. What do you say?"

"That sounds good to me Mike. I will just sit out here a spell and reminisce a little more to myself. This is the first time I have allowed myself the pleasure."

I worked my way through the cupboards and Gus was right. He had a lot of food. He also had enough beef in the freezer to feed a small army. I decided to cook up a little thing of my own. I dug out the spices and some brown rice and went to work. In about an hour I had a good pan of Jambalaya.

I hollered for Gus to wash up and grab us two more cold beers on his way back to the table.

Gus sat down and we dug in. It was a little spicier than I had planned and Gus got up to get us two more Bud Lights. After he chugged most of his beer, he looked at me and pronounced it outstanding. A large belch followed this from both of us, which ended in laughter.

I told him to stay put and made quick work of the dishes.

Gus broke out the poker chips and tried to improve his number of wins. The combination of Jambalaya and beer made it men's night. We traded a few jokes and it was definitely memorable.

I yawned and told Gus I was ready for bed, asking him to excuse me for the evening. I was not as tired as I made myself out to be. I needed to think and darkness afforded me that opportunity. Gus may not have been good at cards, but he was good at "the game". He knew throwing out KG-250 was a hook. He also knew it violated every act to merely mention it outside Fort Meade. I doubted Gus worked for anyone other than Uncle Sam. Maybe he was retired; maybe he was not.

The cool sheets felt good and soon I fell fast asleep.

6. THE ULTIMATE SACRIFICE

Wilson opened his eyes and didn't move. The blackout curtains kept the room dark and obliterated time. How long had he been asleep? Someone else was in the room. Their presence must have awakened him. He couldn't make them out and he wasn't ready to move until he could. He listened for breathing and was certain it was coming from the left. Surprise was on his side if he could get to them to snap their neck or crush their throat; it was all he needed. The problem was distance. When you don't know where the enemy is for certain, any error is in their favor. Quietly, slowly, he turned his head and concentrated in the darkness. His eyes were adjusting.

There was a low growl and two piercing red eyes looked back at him.

"Prince, come here boy," he said with some trepidation. Prince closed his eyes and suddenly appeared at Wilson's right side, like a ghost. He turned on the wall switch illuminating the room. Prince was not there. No one else was either. He knew he had not been dreaming.

Apparently, he had slept so long the sun had been up for hours. He shaved, showered, and dressed in his jeans that were hanging over a chair. Underneath them was a clean tee shirt.

It was time to have that talk with Gus.

He stopped at Gus' bedroom door and knocked lightly. There was no answer so he opened it softly. The bedding appeared it had not been disturbed. He walked out to the kitchen and saw a note on the table.

"Take care of Prince and he will take care of you. 435#*prince789nsa. – Gus".

It looked like Gus had written down his router password. Interesting to see '789' since that was Wilson's I.D. number when he worked at the intelligence agency. All right, well, first he needed breakfast. He fried some bacon, made some toast, cut up a grapefruit, and put on a pot of coffee. Remembering Prince, he put some dog chow from the bag under the sink in his bowl and poured a little of the grease over it. The water dish was empty and by the time he turned around with it full of water, Prince was quietly eating.

Wilson stood there for a minute and marveled at Prince's size. He had to weigh in about 130-140 pounds. For such a big creature, he could move fast and silent. "Like a ghost," Gus had said. He remembered the first time they met and Prince put his paws on his chest, his head was directly at chin level. This would make him stand well over 5' tall on two legs and over 3' on four. His paws were not quite as large as the palm of his hands, but close. Wilson wished he knew his story. Prince backed away from his food and stared at him.

"Oh, the water," Wilson said, "Sorry Prince." He set it down in front of him. As he drank, Wilson grabbed a bottle of water for himself.

He stepped around him and opened the door. When he looked back to see if Prince wanted to go outside, he had disappeared. Wilson was not sure if he had his own way out or in so he left the door ajar. It was a nice morning for a walk and he needed to get out.

Looking around, he did his best to get his bearings with the morning sun and the house. There were not any trees in sight. He studied things for a moment and decided he could find his way back if he did not venture more than a mile or so out. The farther he walked the more he tried to recall the events leading up to someone leaving the note in his car. Someone followed him that night to save his life. Someone had discovered him, someone had given him up and this cost that someone his or her life. He was back to hunting those hunting him again.

He was heating up with the tall crop all around and the sun overhead. The water he had brought was half-gone. It was time to head back. He spent a few minutes getting his bearings again and picking a location where he thought the farmhouse was. Another three hours proved him wrong. He was stuck. The smart thing to do was to hunker down until there was a clear definition when the stars came out. He had marked it in his mind with the Dippers the night Gus and he had sat outside. Next time, he was bringing a compass.

Sitting in the sun was not ideal. Wilson did not know where Prince was, but if Gus had not exaggerated, Prince knew where he was.

He whistled and called. He looked around for any kind of shelter from direct sun but did not see anything. Taking off his tee shirt, he poured the rest of the water on it and draped it over his head. He was thinking how stupid he looked when

Prince pushed against him. He liked this dog more and more. Prince looked up at his head.

Wilson said, "Yeah, I know I look stupid. I'm hot and not ashamed to tell you I'm lost." Prince grabbed his wrist and gave it a tug nearly pulling him down. He had sharp teeth and they cut into his skin. About the time Wilson noted some blood from his contact, Prince let go and began moving out. He followed him at a pace that was faster than a walk and slower than a run. They did this for what seemed like forever before he brought Wilson to the door. He was never so grateful to get inside a house. He was dehydrated, thirsty, and the sweat was pouring off. He pushed the door open and grabbed a glass from the cupboard. Prince was gone by the time he turned around.

He toweled off and made the decision he had been postponing for some time. He needed to get some help. He grabbed a phone from his bag and entered the router number Gus had left in the note.

It sync'd up on the first try and he sent an email to the last address he knew Annie Chavis monitored. He hadn't used it in years. Hell, he didn't even know if she was still alive. Wilson told Chavis he needed her help. He said to reply to their drop box and powered the phone off. It looked like Gus had placed his communications deep within NSA's firewall. Wilson had to think his number 789 would pop, but by the time it was pulled, it had circled the globe so many times, it would take days before even they knew it was him. They were no threat, though. Gus could explain how he was operating within their firewall if it came to that. It was the prison time Wilson worried about. Besides, they could not decode the email message because his code was based on nothing known. He also was confident it would not reveal from where it was actually sent. He was more concerned about what he did not know.

He made a sandwich after feeding Prince and turned on FOX again. FOX had run the news about his house and he hoped they'd run more. After the 12 o'clock news of the day, the follow-up on his house ran. There was a new development. The body was identified as Marine Captain Benjamin Roberts. An unidentified source in local law enforcement said Captain Roberts died from a close gun-shot wound to the head. Shepard Smith said Robert's only family was his 92-year old mother, Bessie, who had died last fall. Smith shook his head and said he doubted this story was over as law enforcement was extremely tight-lipped.

Robbie had been Wilson's Captain and like a brother to him. They served together in the 3rd Marines. He knew he was assigned to the State Department or Department of Defense, or something like that. This story was indeed far from over Shep. Robbie was his Marine Corps family. As soon as Gus returned, he would find out who killed Robbie and take out everyone around them. Locate, Isolate, and Eliminate. LIE. It had been his personal motto in the Corps.

He leaned in with the remote to shut off the TV and saw the picture of Prince again. He wasn't being nosy, but had a feeling Gus wasn't coming back – at least not right away. Recalling his hiding something in it, he lifted it up and opened it. There was a note to him.

"Mike, here is a special device I made to track Prince. You take care of him and he will take care of you. The screen has two buttons. One is for on and the other off. Very simple. On its side is a night switch that changes the LCD glow so it is not visible from the sides. If you tap the screen, Prince will search for you. It sends a signal to his collar."

He put the device back and burned the note in the high temp firebox. It was one of those fireplaces that burned so hot, it emitted no smoke. He was not sure what Gus had in place to take care of the heat signature, but no doubt that had been thought of. Now, he needed to find Gus' computer. If Gus had NSA access, there had to be a computer somewhere.

For hours, he looked and found nothing. He searched under, over, and in just about everything. *Bravo Gus. You hid it well or you took it with you.*

Dinner was rather quiet. Wilson missed having Gus. He ate the leftover spaghetti in silence while Prince ate his chow. They were like two pouting kids not talking to one another. He didn't know if Prince was upset at Gus leaving or upset at being stuck with him. He would eat and stare. Wilson talked to him and re-told the story of Maria disappearing. He didn't give any feedback. After dinner Prince disappeared again. Wilson watched a little TV and decided to go to bed. He pulled out Prince's racking device from the back of the photo where Gus kept it hidden and turned it on. He tapped on the display twice and then watched. Within seconds, it came to life and a small diamond icon began moving towards the house. He powered it off and waited. And waited.

Finally, he got up, opened the door, and looked out. Darkness and stars looked back. He felt a push against his right leg and there was Prince. He hadn't come in the front door. Wilson motioned for him to go on patrol as he had seen Gus do and Prince took off. Wilson felt like Prince knew what he was doing more than Wilson did. He shut the door, locked up, and went to bed.

This time he had left a bedroom blind up a couple inches for the sun to wake him up.

It seemed he had only been asleep a few hours when sun intruded into the room, waking him up. Prince lay sleeping alongside his bed. That was a good sign.

By the time he had eaten, fed Prince, and gotten dressed, he had a hunch where Gus's computer was. In fact, it would explain a lot of things. He walked outside and around the farmhouse. Grabbing a shovel nearby, he dug at a corner and hit concrete. It went down further than he could dig. That meant there was a basement. It also explained how Prince got in and out without being seen.

Wilson spent all day inside the house and could not find a way down. He grabbed a cold Bud Light and sat down in Gus' chair. He pulled the lever for the foot rest and nothing happened. That was strange because he knew Gus had his feet up when he was reading a few nights ago. Wilson looked down and laughed at the teeth marks on it. He pulled on it again and the footrest came up. He pushed the lever back and the footrest folded down. He played with this for a few minutes and it was always the same.

What if he pushed the lever down after pulling it up once and left it down? He tried that and heard a slight noise in the hall. Up, then down opened something. Up, down, up brought the footrest up. Interesting.

He pulled the lever up and put it down. The noise in the hallway was barely discernible. He wondered why he hadn't heard it before but maybe it was because they were always talking. He got up and walked into the hall. Nothing was out of the ordinary. He opened the closet doors to the washer/dryer to find a side panel open, exposing stairs going down. The stairwell was lit so he squeezed through. There was another lever at the bottom. It also had teeth marks on it. He rocked it. The panel to the washer/dryer closed, but the lights stayed on. *Well, well, aren't you full of secrets, Gus?*

There was a large roll top desk along a wall. He rolled up the cover and there was a very modern looking LCD screen looking back at him. There was also a note. It said, "Before I treated your wound, I looked you up and spoke with a friend. I'm at peace. – Gus." Wilson wondered what that was about and how did Gus get access to his clearance? Wilson needed to get into the computer. He powered it up, it flashed "PASSWORD" and Wilson knew he had a one in seven chance of being correct before it locked down. Well, he may as well start with his old one.

It booted up and he had access. Suddenly a digital countdown timer appeared showing there was exactly five-minutes and twenty-nine-seconds left. Whatever that meant, it was more time than he needed. It took a lot of NSA power, but he accessed the Sally Sue computer once more and read quickly.

"A witness from their 14th floor apartment at Pentagon city said a missile came in low like a small fighter jet. In fact that's what she thought it was at first. However, at the last minute it nose-dived, then straightened out and went directly into the side of the Pentagon as if it was controlled. The hole it left was about 70 feet wide in diameter and only went in about 16-feet. The grass had not even been disturbed yet it had skimmed at ground level. The same witness noted that there were no wings, no fuselage, no engines, and no tail – nothing. The fire itself was small. This contrasted against later newspaper stories stating the hole was five stories high and 200 feet wide.

He also knew that the Pentagon was one of the most, if not the most, fortified building in the world. Did anyone honestly believe a 125 foot wide plane caused the hole he was seeing? Only the nose of a Boeing 757 could have penetrated the first three rings at best. When a fire broke out, the nose and wings made of carbon fiber would burn, but the fuselage made of aluminum and the jet engines made of steel would remain as a burned out wreck. Never has there been a plane crash in history, anywhere in the world, where jet fuel turned everything and everyone into ashes.

Many stories surfaced and were in dispute. Some citizens claimed to have seen the plane hit. Maybe they did. Other conspiracy theorists noted two large construction trailers parked at that opening prior to the explosion were obliterated and must have had the airplane parts that were "found" inside.

One thing was for sure. No one or agency every verified the tail number to flight A77, N644AA, or any other plane. For the first time in our modern aviation history, there was no attempt at reconstruction. No body parts or other identifiers were located.

What was going on here and why had the government hidden this?

Wilson scanned several pages reading one that ended, "… had not anticipated the plane sticking into the side of the tower and not passing through to the third tower. Imploding the third tower could not be stopped as charges on all stories had been activated by computer sequence."

He signed off before the clock ended and powered things off. Everyone remembered the controversy and uproar days later when Americans began to question the logic of how could the third tower turned to dust when nothing struck it.

Metallurgic and structure experts said that building was brought down by charges carefully placed under each floor. This led to many demanding an examination of the other buildings. Kerosene (airplane fuel) did not burn hot enough to change the properties of steel into a fine powder. The government put a lot of disinformation out, then clamped a lid on it and like the Kennedy assassination, it soon went away.

Was it this information that Maria had seen that caused her disappearance? 9/11 debriefing analysis, photos, presidential notes? Some people have lived shorter lives knowing less about secrets. This was not a healthy area to involve himself in unless he needed to be. He had to be careful. The CIA had a lot of manpower. Most of them were not as good as him; and a few were even better. What Wilson needed was to find Maria and make the price for whoever took her, beyond what they were willing to sacrifice. He was not sure if he could do that alone. He left the desk and stretched.

The room was worth exploring so he paced it off. It was larger than the main house. There was a very large walk-in safe that he was sure was beyond his powers to open. Who knew what Gus had in there. There were cupboards of dried foods, various sundries, extra clothing, shoes and boots in unopened shoeboxes, and a lot of electrical equipment in various boxes. It was a mini general store. He found a medical supply cabinet and a small refrigerator with serums. Gus was well prepared to sit things out here for a few years.

In the corner was an over sized chair and a TV. He plopped down in it. The problem with having access to secrets is one that could get caught up in too many of them and be overwhelmed. One would also be put down quicker than a rabid pit-bull outside a church on a Sunday morning for creating "problems" as they say.

To Wilson that meant that it went higher than this nation should know. It also meant that its answer would remain protected for life. 9/11 was large. The Public would never know the truth, could never know. Period.

Maria. *Where are you?* He had let them distract him with collateral damage. They could not bring the fight to him directly so they made sure it was all around him. They kept him busy running and hiding. This gave them time to interrogate Maria. They needed to find out what she knew and whom she may have shared that information with. They needed a safe place where he could not reach her. Langley itself was off-limits for that sort of thing; Camp Perry was not.

Camp Perry was the Armed Forces Experimental Training Activity base outside Williamsburg, Virginia. It consisted of 9,000 acres. It also was known as "the Farm", the CIA training facility. Another little piece of land in Hertford, North Carolina known to some as "the Point" was the "sister Farm". He was betting they didn't know he knew about the Point. Maria would most likely be there. So would he.

That night he fed Prince his chow, gave him some fresh water and told him they were going to have a chat after dinner. Wilson made himself a steak, found a bottle of Black Jack Daniels and thought about how he could get out of the Point. Getting into any secure place was always easier than getting out. Getting in was unexpected; leaving was not always so pleasant. Often, unfriendlies were waiting.

He cleaned up and looked for Prince. He appeared behind him without warning and Wilson sent him out on patrol. They would start in the morning after breakfast. Wilson put the Jack away and went to bed.

Prince was lying down in the bedroom doorway when he woke up. Wilson shaved, showered, and dressed and they ate. Prince let Wilson place his hands on him for the first time. He rubbed his head, scratched his ears and then told him they needed to train. He was under no illusions that Prince understood him.

They went outside he started working with him using hand signals. Prince allowed Wilson to maneuver him most of the time. When he didn't like it, he flashed his teeth to let him know. Wilson would slow down and use more patience when Prince did this. He was a quick learner.

He had the feeling that Prince knew some of these commands already. Prince definitely had a propensity to learn tactics quickly. He was great at crawling; he was very adept at finding and bringing the .45 to him, no matter where it was hidden; and he knew how to disappear when signaled to do so. It was a good start. After nearly four hours, Wilson was exhausted.

It was a great start, and tomorrow they would accomplish even more if Prince was willing. Wilson told him patrol and he took off.

The kitchen still needed cleaning from breakfast and he went to work before sitting down with a Bud Light. He took some chicken out to thaw for dinner and caught the last of FOX News with Shep. There was no mention of Robbie or his house.

He looked through some of the books in the bookcase and found a large Rand McNalley road atlas with the best route to Hertford, North Carolina highlighted. He smiled to himself. He thought again, *I do not believe in coincidences. There are none.*

Gus's property was about 150-miles or less as the crow flies from "the Point", or "Harvey Point"; also known as the "second Farm". The National Forest would get him there or within a stone's throw.

He spent the rest of his afternoon, plotting, drafting alternate routes based on what if's, and finding known sources of water in the area. This was just a "hike" for him. Maria jogged every morning so she should be able to handle the physical part. He just did not know what kind of shape she would be in and if she could do what he needed her to do when he brought her out. This would be a delicate operation. Breaking into their camp was one thing. Stealing a "package" and terminating security to do this would cause meetings. His boss would want an explanation before removing the bounty off his head. Wilson was sure they were doing their best to feed his boss misinformation on a daily basis about him. With his being off the grid there was no way he could be reached. He had to be patient. However, when you are the big boss, patience only lasted so long. This was starting to play out on TV in unrelated stories.

* * *

This was going to be his last night to eat heavy. He fried up the chicken that had thawed out, made some mashed potatoes, and whipped up homemade gravy. His mom would be proud. Feeling guilty, he heated up some green beans with butter. All right, now his mom would be proud. Prince was happy too. He loved the gravy on his chow.

Wilson ate more than one person should and cleaned up. It took longer to clean the kitchen than it did to make dinner. He was not certain about keeping the leftovers so he took them out to the shaft Gus had for garbage.

He needed to get a good night's sleep but knew it would not happen just yet. He settled for a book he found on the 9/11 Commission's investigation. There were in fact several books devoted to that subject. Gus must have had some questions too and had some interesting reading on hand.

When the book had fallen out of his hands twice, Wilson decided it was time for bed. He pulled out the Prince device and tapped it twice, then put it back and continued to read. Prince appeared almost 30 minutes later. He was panting heavily in between drinking water and cooling down. Once he appeared rested, Wilson sent him back on patrol for the night. He locked up and went to bed, leaving the bedroom door open.

Daylight crept down the hall before waking him up. Prince lay once again at the foot of the bed. It made him feel good. They made short work of their morning routine and they stepped outside. They practiced yesterday's signals. If there were any mistakes, they were Wilson's. It took less than an hour. He spent the next three hours teaching Prince to drag him, carry his quick bag, and parallel his hiking, all by signal. Prince's favorite seemed to be point man. Wilson would send him out, wait, and on cue, every twelve minutes he would return. Six minutes out and six minutes back. Lie down; crawl backwards if a threat appeared. They practiced this until both of them were tired. It was a little difficult to establish what a "threat" was by sign language and get Prince to ignore it. Wilson did not have confidence in this one. He suspected Prince would want to attack instead of return. He certainly had extensive training in protection duty before Wilson's arrival. Taking him off property would be a new routine. They would see.

They ate a little earlier than usual. Wilson made a boring salad and poured himself a large water. Prince got his chow but without anything extra. It did not seem to bother him. Maybe both of them were wrapping their minds around this mission. He certainly hoped so.

After dinner, Wilson cleaned up and headed into the basement. He needed to know the buildings and their layouts at "the Point." He was not sure where to start, but it would be a computer search.

He powered it on and waited for PASSWORD to flash. It took the old one again and the clock started. He had five minutes and twenty-nine seconds. He could have looked first at the CIA but he did not want them to know he was coming. Instead, he looked at the National Archives Building construction and a couple NSA satellite over head feeds of Hertford, North Carolina. When he found what he wanted, the clock flashed 59 seconds. He committed to memory all that he could. When he opened the last set of over-heads, he found a building marked "Infirmary". Bingo. The clock flashed three seconds and he powered off completely. He had what was needed. If Maria was not there, he was screwed and she would be dead. Maybe they all would be dead.

Prince was sent on patrol and he locked up before going to bed to get a couple hours sleep. He was not sure he even dozed off and was up at midnight. He left a note for Gus that did not say much except that he had Prince with him.

Again, he had a nagging feeling Gus had told him as much as he had because he was not coming back. That was another puzzle itself, but he did not have time to think about it.

After he was armed and had grabbed his quick bag and compass, Prince joined him. They headed to the Jeep. Moving at night seemed to make the journey shorter. He was excited and ready. He could only hope by the time he reached "the Point" he would feel the same. He sat the bag down and turned the pump. There was the familiar swoosh and an area of crops disappeared against the sky, followed by the rise of the Jeep. Wilson loaded it up and jumped in. Prince did not want to get in. He cajoled and ordered but Prince just backed away even more. Wilson wasn't sure if he could do it without him, but it's what he had to do and he was good at it. Just as he was backing up, he saw Prince leap into the rear seat. Wilson did not hesitate, but put it in gear, powered on the fancy navigational screen, and headed out.

Using four-wheel drive, they climbed slowly, mostly by compass to get into the U.S. Forest and visually to bypass some heavily treed areas. Where possible they came down onto ranger or logging access roads. They had traveled for hours. About ten miles out from Hertford, Wilson found a place to put the jeep that afforded what he thought would be hidden from the sky and the road. There was a mining cave that had been widened at the mouth probably to bring in supplies many years ago. He was able to back into it and cover up the front. Carefully, he marked it on his digital compass and noted the time. He studied where the moon lit up in relation to its location. If he could not find it on his way back, he owed Gus or somebody a Jeep.

He grabbed his gear and Prince jumped off. Prince waited and looked for the signal. Wilson lifted his arm straight out like they had practiced and pointed. Prince took off. Wilson didn't move, but instead timed him. He was back in twelve minutes. He was going to do his part and now Wilson needed to do his. They continued like this until they got within 2,500 feet of "the Point". Generally, agencies liked to get vibration sensors in and around their properties at about 2,500 feet from their fence line. The CIA was no different. At 1,000 feet Wilson expected audio and at the fence line, there would be video. In addition, there would be scout teams outside the fence. These would be the "armed" response teams. The fun thing was that they consisted of the trainees. The agency was never really concerned about breaches. They kept no secrets here. More importantly, the internal security was real. The exterior was meant to deprive trainees of sleep and, pardon the pun, *spook* them from time to time with fake abductions or kills.

The duty officer never was told because they wanted all teams to respond accordingly for the practice and maybe, someday, the real thing. Tonight they were about to have one of their unscheduled drills.

In Wilson's bag, he had what was called a "reader." It located any electronic device known that sent signals. He had put it to use getting into unfriendly locations many times. He pulled out the reader, did a scan and took a bearing with his compass. Prince waited. Wilson pointed at a tree to his right at 90 degrees and Prince took off, followed by Wilson. They continued in this manner for the next seven minutes when the reader emitted a warning. Both vibration and audio showed in the area. That was interesting. They were still well over 1,500 feet out. He signaled Prince to hide and he blended into the ground with ground cover. Company would be coming.

Having an armed team come out gave him an opportunity to not only time, but also observe their response. It was under three minutes. These guys were thorough too. They got out of a Hummer and walked the area using hand signals. They moved the vehicle and doubled-back quietly on foot to wait. They waited thirty minutes, then left. This was a mixed blessing.

It made getting in and out very improbable, but it confirmed to Wilson that there was something or someone inside they wanted to keep.

He pulled out his device and tapped the screen twice for Prince to return. Prince appeared out of nowhere and they moved back. As he was doing so, Wilson clapped his hands loudly twice together.

This time when they came there was a senior agent and a recruit. Prince walked out and got their attention. They did as trained; the senior guard moved behind the Hummer aiming an assault rifle and the recruit removed a .45 from his holster. The one with the .45 approached Prince. Wilson sprang. As soon as he had the senior guard on the ground and rendered unconscious, he taped his mouth, and cuffed him. He looked up to see that Prince somehow had disarmed the guard with the .45. He was holding him by the throat. Gus had said he was good with guns. The recruit appeared too scared to move. They had not practiced this catch and release part. Wilson signaled Prince to keep the rifleman prone and walked over to the recruit. He had pissed his pants he was so scared. His throat was bleeding slightly from punctures.

Wilson walked over and picked him up wiping the bloody slobber from his throat. He didn't want to kill any of these guys unless it was necessary. He could see the recruit was bewildered.

"Look, not only are you out of the game, but you can be terminated due to poor performance. I have the power to save your job. How you perform for me for the rest of the event is up to you. This is a drill. You could make up for your 'dying' tonight," said Wilson.

He eyed Wilson warily.

"We have all the intel we needed; you just have to be my driver and stay with me until the duty officer calls things to a halt."

"What is it that I am supposed to do?" he asked, with the hope of keeping his job clearly in his eyes.

"What's your name?"

"Rogers," he replied.

"Well, first thing, Rogers, is we take the Hummer and return to base. "We'll leave your partner for the duty command to pick him up. He's screwed. I'll anchor him in place because some of these guys cheat".

Wilson dragged the rifleman over behind a tree near his quick bag containing the tools he needed. Chaining his ankles, he staked him to the ground. He also took his uniform and boots and putting them on while Prince kept the recruit company. The boots were a little tight, but they'd do. He presented himself after grabbing his quick bag and motioned Prince to hide and wait before walking over to the recruit. Prince ran off.

"You drive," Wilson said. "I'm going to kick back. At the gate just do what you normally do and drive in. Let's head to the infirmary. We'll get you cleaned up and a shot for that bite, then meet up with the rest of my team where you will be assigned tonight."

Wilson was improvising but he thought it bold enough to work.

He put his quick bag on the rear floor of the Hummer before climbing into the passenger seat and pulled his hat down low over his face. He sighed and stretched his legs out as if he were bored. The recruit started the vehicle and radioed that they were returning.

They entered through a side gate manned by another recruit. The two recruits waved at each other like the classmates they were. *Where did they get these guys?* Wilson wondered. There appeared to be no movement within the compound. It was still dark but wouldn't be for long. He had to move fast and hope luck remained on his side.

"Rogers, have you ever worked that gate we came in?"

"Yes, I have. Just last night."

"What's that recruit's name we passed and what is the normal protocol needed to exit?"

Rogers replied giving Wilson what he needed for his way back out. Then he added, if they drove right up to the infirmary tonight, the agents there would know something was wrong.

"Why would they know that?" Wilson asked. "What were your orders?"

"All recruits were told the infirmary was off limits unless they had the duty officer's written permission or someone was with them. There's no way around that as all the people there are wearing these really cool looking black uniforms."

Wilson knew black unis were fully trained security guards that failed agent training and offered a position elsewhere. Many took it so they could say they worked "for the government" sounding mysterious and impressing their girlfriends.

"Your job is to tell me where I can get one of those black uniforms then, Rogers."

"I don't know," he said.

"Well, how about the laundry? There has to be a laundry on base, right?"

"Yes sir. Sorry, I didn't think about that."

They headed over there first. He asked Rogers to park on the fenced side and wait. Rogers said that a patrol came by every seven minutes and if they parked there, sentries would stop to investigate. If he parked by the building, fence patrol passing by would investigate too, or alert the duty officer.

"Good thinking. Drop me nearby and come back by every four to five minutes until I jump in."

"Yes sir."

Wilson kept low and hugged the base cleaners. There were no visible alarms. He forced open a back door and went inside. It took him a couple minutes to change into a starched black uni that had the rank of Major on the epaulets. There was a fabric gun belt and holster for a .45 hanging on its hook as well. Someone was going to be very unhappy in the morning. Just as he finished, the fence patrol came by and he ducked down. They didn't even look over his way. Fence patrol to these guys meant just that, he laughed to himself.

Rogers brought the hummer back by and stopped. He looked twice before he realized it was Wilson coming out the door.

"I thought you were someone else," he said, "Sir, if I may make a suggestion about the infirmary?"

"What?"

"It's where I work when I'm not on guard duty. I just started my training to be a corpsman. Officers always come in the side door – never the front. Perhaps we should enter that way."

Rogers had turned out to be his key. Wilson hoped he could keep him alive. He had earned it so far.

"Alright. Good thought. By the way do they have any beds in there or rooms with cots?" Wilson asked.

"If anyone is that sick, they call for a helicopter and take them out. Although, there was someone brought in for quarantine recently. The whole thing was weird. They brought them in late one afternoon. Their head was wrapped hiding their face. They half carried them downstairs and immediately we were told the infirmary was off limits."

"What was weird about that?" Wilson asked.

"I thought if it was for quarantine, why wasn't anyone wearing masks or suits? Moreover, why were we allowed to remain on the premises? I was a little uneasy about it until Doc took me aside and said it was part of interrogation training. It was right after that a helo arrived with guys wearing black uniforms. They took over our building. They're not very friendly guys either. I mean, like you sir, you're obviously a ranking officer and with all due respect sir, you seem like a pretty decent guy."

Wilson put his .45 in the empty holster and his silenced .22 in the large leg pocket of his black uniform before telling Rogers to move out. He had done some training in Williamsburg at "the Farm" with Langley boys and had a few missions with them. They pulled up and parked. He brought Rogers in through the side door with him, passing one guard who glared, put his hand on his gun until he saw the rank, then looked away. Wilson stopped and asked him for identification. He produced a plasticized card that said his name was Thomas Kresse. Wilson told Rogers to have the night corpsman treat his wounds and get a tetanus shot reminding him he was not to discuss their business. He was instructed to meet back here when he was ready.

"Kresse, you're with me," Wilson said, "Which way is downstairs?"

Kresse took him back towards the entrance they had come in from and pointed down a hall. Wilson told him Langley had decided to take a different direction. He was to follow his orders exactly.

"Do you understand that, Kresse? Do exactly what you are told," Wilson said.

"Yes sir," he replied.

Wilson told him to go down the stairs in front of him. The room was much bigger than he had envisioned. When he got down there, he was very surprised by who he saw. Sending Kresse ahead probably saved his life. No one saw the surprise look on his face. One guard sat at a table playing solitaire. A nurse was at a desk in the corner writing. He wanted to kill both of them, but he didn't. If he made it out of there alive, he didn't want to give anyone the excuse that he should go to prison or be killed. He had no illusions both of those were in play now, but he hoped his boss would countermand all of those when he heard the story.

The guard was on his feet as soon as he recognized the rank of Major. Wilson motioned Kresse to come closer and quickly knocked them both out and down. He turned around and found the nurse running for the stairs. Just as she started to yell, he crushed her larynx with a kick harder than he hoped it would be. It was reflex on his part – survival mode. He heard some movement upstairs and walked over to the stairwell. When the door opened, he casually walked up to see guns pointed towards him.

"Put those away," Wilson ordered, "We're just having a little disagreement down here."

He saw Rogers' head above the second guard and Rogers smiled. They closed the door. It was hard coming back from any interrogation, especially if you had not trained for them. He found a water bottle and a clean cloth. He pressed a button to raise the bed and removed the catheter and first aid tape. There was a groan and a flicker of the eyelids.

They had to get moving.

"Jeff, are you alright? Can you move? We need to get you out of here, buddy. Right now!"

Jeff Tompkins was pretty weak. He and Kresse were about the same height so Wilson dressed him in Kresse's uniform, boots and all. Jeff's eyes glazed over. Some sort of shock had set in, but he was moving. Wilson pulled the cap down over Tompkins' eyes and helped him to his feet.

They went up the stairs and found two guards with Rogers at the top, waiting on the main floor. He nodded to Rogers and passed Jeff off to him saying this man was sick and he was taking him on the helo back with him to Langley.

He asked for I.D. from both guards, Gnirk and Cavelti. He told Gnirk to return to his post and discuss this with no one. He told Cavelti to stand guard at the door with instructions that no one was to go in or out until the command duty officer relieved him. He walked out and helped Rogers lay Jeff on the rear seat of the Hummer. The sun was starting to break. More time had passed than he had thought. They climbed in and headed back to the side gate. Luckily the change of the guard had not taken place. The recruit staffing the gate smiled, flagged Rogers to a stop and exchanged verbal code. He looked at Wilson and waved them through. Wilson was not sure how they were going to explain Jeff lying on the back seat, but the guard's inattention to detail was all he needed.

He directed Rogers to drive well outside the safe zone, in the opposite direction he was going. They were about 3,000 feet out before he told him to stop and pointed in the direction of the area where they first met.

"Okay Rogers, one last assignment before the night's over. Walk straight in that direction and you should come across where we first made contact. If your partner has not been picked up yet, untie him and head back in. If he's no longer there, same thing – head back in. Your duty officer will be expecting you."

Wilson, smiled, reached out, shook his hand, and thanked him. He actually meant it. The guy was an idiot. He waited until he walked off and drove the Hummer away. After five minutes, he pulled out the digital device and tapped it twice for Prince. There was no signal. Wilson waited another five minutes, but he never came. He didn't want to leave him, but he had Jeff to think about and he couldn't risk them getting their hands on him again. He drove off quickly.

Suddenly, the Claxton horns began going off. The whole camp was alert now. They would pull out all stops. He hadn't seen a helo but it didn't mean that there wasn't one parked somewhere. Every vehicle would be coming for them. He hadn't found a place to ditch the Hummer yet, but it was time to leave it. He shut it off and heard a waterfall. Jeff was awake and able to talk a little. He helped him out of the vehicle and set him on the ground with his quick bag before running to the sound of the waterfall. He found it and saw it cascading several feet into a lake below. He came back and seconds later, he sent the Hummer over as well. He was hoping it would sink before they arrived in the area.

When he came back, Jeff was sitting up. He gave him a little more water and told him they had to get going if he wanted to live. Jeff could walk but it was like walking with Wilson's grandmother – if he had one. He would only slow them down and they could not afford to lose more time. They stopped and he checked his compass before he placed Jeff in a firefighters' carry and the quick bag in the other hand. It was going to be difficult. There were nearly eight miles to hike. He was loaded down and some pretty angry people were right behind him.

Wilson figured the main focus would be on the lower ground and if they had a helo, it would cover the higher elevation. They knew he would have to carry their prisoner. Hoping the main search would be at the low elevation, he went high. It took a lot of effort to get up the shale and treed mountainside. Once at the top, he had to rest. He squatted and set his bag down. Sweat poured off him and he rolled Jeff off as gently as possible hearing a muffled thank-you.

Jeff tried to smile. He wasn't sure what they had done to him and he wasn't in any condition to have a long conversation. They had to move out. Wilson needed to get them a little higher. This time rolling Jeff onto Wilson's shoulders was harder and picking up the bag was an effort. He was getting tired. He checked his compass and moved upwards in the direction he needed to go. The sun was fully up and there wasn't anywhere to hide if they got close. Making an effort not to crack a branch or send a rock sliding down fatigued him even more. Sweat was pouring down his chest and his back now. His shirt was clinging. He needed to stay hydrated but did not have a lot of time to stop and do that. He pushed himself into a cadence, sounding off silently to himself, and this time covered a lot of ground. They were almost at the top. Wilson heard the enemy before he saw him.

"Stop where you are. Turn around, face me, and set the prisoner down." A guard with a sniper rifle was about ten feet away. There was no way Wilson could get to him before dying. He noted that the rifle had a noise suppressor on it. It was expensive gear and if this guard was carrying one, chances were high that he was combat trained. He also was very calm.

"One more time. Set the prisoner down. My orders are to take you alive if possible, but I will not take any risks to do so."

Repeating the command cost him the moment. Wilson was under no illusions that if he gave his life Jeff would get away, but he was considering it. He kneeled and rolled Jeff off when he heard the hit.

There was no mistaking the force, the snarling, human agony, and the terrible sound of tearing flesh. Jeff was on the ground and Wilson was back on his feet.

Prince had killed the sniper. It definitely looked like a wild animal had gotten this one. No man – or dog - would get the "credit" for it and that was fine by Wilson.

"Well, Prince glad to have you back."

Wilson took a few minutes to remove the rifle's firing pin and set the bloody rifle back down with the body. An animal would not take the rifle, but he couldn't just leave a perfectly good weapon behind his back either.

He signaled Prince to take point, rolled Jeff back onto his shoulders and grabbed his bag. He was running on adrenaline now and needed to get going. Luckily, most of the remaining terrain was level before heading down.

They stopped momentarily when a helo passed over. Wilson couldn't see it, but he knew a stealth Blackhawk UH-60 when he heard the *silent* rotor sound. They were up and hunting. Having access to a stealth bird told him this was being directed at the highest level of government. He promised to find out who in due time.

Prince never slowed. He was back and forth checking in, being praised, until Wilson was almost horse. They were probably about two miles from the Jeep when Wilson had to rest. He rolled Jeff off and dropped his bag. Prince had not come back. He was trained to do so and indicate any human activity although they hadn't had anyone to actually fulfill the bad-guy part. So far, Prince had done a really great job. Wilson hydrated himself and Jeff and made the decision to scout out Prince. He pulled out his sniper rifle from the bag and assembled it, chambering a round as he stood up. He still had the .45 and the silenced .22.

A good sniper finds the best point and lies for hours, sometimes days. He didn't have that luxury. He knew the drill, but this time he had to keep moving. He looked back and used his compass to mark where Jeff was before setting off on a silent jog. He knew approximately where Prince was. He didn't know the speed at which Prince covered ground so he wasn't sure how far out Prince would be or if something took Prince in another direction. He lost about 15-minutes of time looking. Fifteen minutes out, fifteen minutes back meant they would have gained a half hour moving on him. He started to turn back when he saw a flash. That was the nice thing about the sun and someone not being properly trained. There were two guards in black. One held a rifle. He followed the rifle out and it was pointed at Prince who lay on the ground. Wilson shot both of them. Head shots.

He ran for Prince believing the worst. *C'mon on boy. Get up.* It was then he spotted the helo setting in the clearing. Wilson turned and took out the pilot. He could only hope the pilot hadn't used the radio. Wilson had never flown one of the stealth birds, but he knew it held a signal beacon. He ran for it and opened the door, dragging the dead pilot out. It took him a few minutes to find the signal beacon but he couldn't open it without some gear that was back with his quick bag.

He picked it up and turned back to where Prince lay. He was gone. Wilson didn't have time to think about it anymore than he must be okay. There was some blood, but it had probably come from those he attacked.

He ran back to Jeff's location. The rest had done him some good. He was alert. Wilson opened his bag and removed his Corps K-bar knife. He popped the box and cut the transmitter. It took another few minutes to bury it. He disassembled his rifle and put it back in the bag.

"Can you walk Jeff?"

Jeff drank some water and nodded. They started off walking slowly. Wilson was relieved be carrying just his bag. Jeff passed out after about 500 feet and he rolled him onto his shoulders. His compass showed they had gotten off direction and Wilson corrected it by heading left before moving out. He soon found himself in a familiar area. The mineshaft was ahead. Unfortunately, so was company.

Wilson didn't see them. He didn't hear them. Prince, however, suddenly appeared and came out of nowhere at a run, tipping him off. He reacted exactly as they had worked on when danger was in front of Wilson. He then disappeared. Wilson retreated into the woods a bit and set Jeff and the bag down. He pulled out his sniper rifle and assembled it once again. He moved back to their original location. Just as he was raising it to have a look, there was whump behind him and he turned to see Prince was crushing a guards' neck.

He looked through his scope to see two spotters and a sniper moving into the mineshaft. He took out all three. At this point, he didn't care about who or how many he killed to get out of there. He didn't care if he shot them in the front or in the back. He had tried minimal damage and it hadn't worked. Now, they were running for their lives. He looked back and signaled Prince to move to the mine.

Prince disobeyed and ran back into the woods. Jeff. Something either had Jeff or was back there. Wilson came in from the side with his rifle cradled and saw a guard in a black unis holding a knife in front of Jeff's throat. Prince was nowhere around.

"Drop your rifle or I take him out before you can shoot me," said the guard.

Wilson smiled. It was the last thing he said before Wilson shot him dead. Shooting from a cradled arm had been a hobby of his that he honed in the Marines. When he was given a Remington XM2010 to test, he never gave it back. It's what he carried now and he was obviously pretty good with it.

Jeff fell on his hands and knees before standing up. He drank some more water. Wilson told him he needed to clear an area and he would be back. Jeff sat down.

Wilson had two choices. He could go in the mineshaft now or he could wait outside awhile and then go in. Either way, he had to go in. Since time was not on his side, he decided to enter now. Just as he was approaching from the side, there came a terrible agonizing muffled moan from inside and one gunshot. Prince came out, took one look at him, and moved in a half-walk, half-run in Jeff's direction.

Things were clear now. Wilson went in and found the three guys he shot and what was left of someone that had been hiding under his Jeep. He knelt down and saw this guy had been in the middle of connecting a timer and C4 to the starter. Wilson removed it and left it behind.

He started the Jeep and drove over to Jeff who was just walking out of the woods. He helped him in. Prince took two tries to jump into the back. Even he was tired. Wilson tossed in the "quick" bag. They took off as the navigation screen powered up. He was convinced if they could get back on the ranch they would be safe. The only passable road to the mine came from the opposite direction so if anyone else were coming by land, that's the direction they would come from. It also was the one they could not take now.

He put the Jeep in low and it crawled up and over similar terrain to what they they used to get here. Wilson himself had crawled, walked, run, and fought for the past ten miles. He was beat. It was mid-morning. They had almost one-hundred miles left to go. Where he could, he sped up. Around 4 in the afternoon, they had reached the end of the National Forest. He was elated; Jeff had been unconscious most of the way.

He drove onto the property and began the trek to the pump. He jumped out and set Prince on patrol. Prince went but seemed to lack his usual enthusiasm. He was tired. Wilson understood. He rotated the pump and jumped back into the Jeep. While the system was doing its thing, he remembered Gus' reply to him about carrying in groceries. He suspected --hoped -- there was tunnel access to the house.

The Jeep moved down into a cavern that was well lit. It was cool and dry. The ceiling re-sealed itself overhead. He saw a six foot flat cargo cart similar to something from a Home Depot, to the side of the Jeep and he lay Jeff on it. He grabbed his quick bag and pushed the cart down the tunnel for a long time. Maybe he had made a mistake and this was an escape tunnel to another part of the property. He finally came to a walled end and large red button on a T-bar. He pushed it. Nothing happened. He pulled it. Still nothing happened. He pushed, pulled, pushed again and the wall slipped open. He found himself in Gus's basement. The wall containing the bookcase and fireplace had moved aside. The floor had. an elaborate roller system.

He rolled Jeff onto his shoulder and grabbed his bag to walk inside. The floor moved on its own and the wall closed. He looked back. Had he not known he'd come out that way, he never would have thought it opened.

He took Jeff up and lay him on Gus's bed. Jeff's breathing was labored. Wilson needed to get an IV into him. He suspected getting his fluid level up would be the most important step. Downstairs in the medical area, he found what he needed. There were a couple of saline bags in the medical refrigerator, inside a special temperature tray. He grabbed one and rigged up a drip system into his veins. Jeff should be better in a couple hours.

A shower sounded pretty good. After he scrubbed himself pink and stood in the cold water for what seemed like another twenty minutes, he toweled off and got dressed. He poked his head in on Jeff and he was still out. His breathing sounded better. Wilson realized he hadn't eaten in almost 24 hours. He was starved.

He couldn't wait for a steak to thaw. Since he had thrown out all the leftovers, he had to settle for a peanut butter and jelly sandwich. He ate two. When Wilson looked up, he saw Prince standing there. The door was not open, but he knew he had his own way in and out. Wilson filled up the chow dish and set down fresh water. Prince stepped forward and collapsed. Wilson kneeled down and didn't see any reason for it. It took a lot to roll him over. When he did, he found he had been shot in two places. The blood had coagulated so it must have been early on in their fight. Wilson opened Prince's mouth and it was full of blood. His breathing was very shallow. He was dying.

He grabbed the compass and his .45, and rolled Prince across his shoulders like he had carried Jeff earlier. There was no time to try to find out how to open the floor to the tunnel. He marked his direction and jogged the best he could to the pump for the jeep. He had some medical training and he had saved some lives, but he was under no illusions about saving Prince. Wilson arrived at the pump before he realized it. He set Prince down gently. He swung the pump around and when the Jeep surfaced, he got Prince into the back seat. He powered up the navigational system and looked for the town that Gus had taken him into before setting at off at high speed.

The doors of Penny's store were locked when he arrived and a car pulled in behind him as he turned around. It was Penny.

"What happened? Is Gus okay?" she asked getting out of the car.

"Is there a pet or doctor in town?" Wilson asked, pointing to Prince.

"We have a doctor, yes. Follow my car, it will be quicker."

Wilson backed up and followed her down the road, turning left onto a smaller road. They drove through an area where probably most of the town lived before stopping at a small brown house. Penny jumped out of her car and ran to the porch yelling, "Dr. Rhinehart. Doc – we need help out here." She pounded on the door.

Wilson saw a white male about 70-years old hurry out and down the porch. He waved him over to the Jeep. This man appeared to know Prince and ever so tenderly, lifted up his huge head. Prince was lifeless.

"He's shutting down. Who did this to him? What the hell happened?" asked the doc gruffly. He looked at Wilson and waited.

"I think he's been shot twice from what I could tell. I had no idea. It must have happened earlier and I let him run around the property. When he showed up for dinner, he collapsed."

"You let him run around or you told him to 'patrol'?" the doc asked.

"I told him to patrol." Wilson felt ashamed the minute he spoke those words.

He had been so concerned about he and Jeff, he didn't apply the same thought to Prince. "Take care of Prince and he will take care of you". That is what Gus had said to him. He trusted him with Prince's life.

"Leave young man. Let me hold him while I can. He is home now. We will take care of him and be with him until his last breath. I would rather you not be here any longer."

Wilson looked over at Penny and she looked away. No doubt, she felt the same.

A sadness came over Wilson, he couldn't explain. Usually, he compartmentalized his feelings. This bothered him the most because there probably had been time to save Prince's life and he hadn't even bothered to check him. Looking back, all the clues were there. He thought Prince was just tired when he half-walked, half-ran; he thought the blood on the ground where Prince had laid was from others. Moreover, when he sent him on patrol, Prince hesitated before he went.

Prince had needed him and he failed him. He had also failed Maria so far.

He had mixed feelings about leaving Prince. Prince should be buried on the property. He struggled in the moment. Jeff needed him.

He told the doc that he had to get back and take care of someone else that was dying.

"Is he shot too?"

"No, it's a long story but someone withheld food and water from him for a long time."

"Maybe you should take me to him," he said.

Wilson told him that was not possible right now; maybe in a day or two he would bring him here. He asked to take Prince back with him.

"Not now," Doc said. "Not now. Give us our time with him. I raised Prince by hand. I have not seen him in almost two years. I am responsible for giving him to Gus. I thought I was doing the right thing."

Tears streamed down his face and he slumped over. Penny walked over and hugged Doc. Wilson heard her break down and they cried together. He could do nothing more here so he left.

The drive home was lonely and longer than it should have been. He crossed the ranch by the barn in darkness. By the time he got back to the pump, nighttime had fallen. He just felt empty. He jumped out, turned the pump sideways and jumped back on the jeep. The walk down the tunnel was not victorious this time. He worked the T-bar to get inside.

He wiped his eyes and the tears from his cheeks. He walked upstairs and looked in on Jeff. He changed the saline bag and reduced its flow. Jeff should be alert in the morning unless there were complications he couldn't see.

Wilson didn't feel like eating anything, but he thought a drink was in order, maybe two. He set out to save Maria, found Jeff, and let Prince die. He poured a couple fingers of Jack Daniels, turned on TV, and fell asleep.

7. KIDNAPPING AN FBI AGENT

Wilson heard someone in the room and opened his eyes to bright sunlight and a smiling Jeff Tompkins. Jeff was holding his hand over where the IV had been connected.

"Well," he said, "When you come after someone, you don't let any moss grow under your feet, do you?"

Wilson laughed and sat up on his elbows. It was good to have a friend again.

"How are you feeling? Can I make you breakfast?"

"I'd feel a lot better if I could shower and maybe borrow some clothes."

"Alright. Come with me and I'll set you up."

He got out of bed and Tompkins followed him down the hall to Gus's room where there were extra clothes. They were not exactly out of G.Q. but they were clean.

While Jeff showered, Wilson made them breakfast. When Jeff finished getting dressed, he sat down and ate until there was no more.

Wilson asked if Jeff felt up to doing the dishes and he headed to the shower. He was feeling down again. No matter what he tried, he could not wash away his guilt about Prince. It nagged at him. He dressed and came back out to the main room.

"Where's that big wolf you had or was I delusional?" Jeff asked.

"You were in and out after I pulled you away from those guys. Speaking of that, what was that all about?"

Jeff sat down across from him and locked eyes for a long-time. A serious look washed over his face.

"Wilson, we need to be straight with each other. I have no idea where I am. I have to trust that your rescuing me was not part of those guys' plans. Out of nowhere, you show up like Superman. I need to contact my office. If you were not part of this, you will let me do that. The Bureau will swing into gear and track these assholes down."

"Jeff, let's put our heads together and talk this out. Maria disappeared while working for our government. You represent the FBI and you disappeared trying to find her. Unless the Bureau is involved, they think you are dead due to a car accident. I lost a friend when I rescued you. Someone has to answer for those things. Someone ordered Maria's pick-up, and then yours. This someone has a lot of juice. They can make things happen."

"I guess my first question Wilson, is how did you know they took me and the second would be, how did you know where to look?"

"I was looking for Maria. I thought you were dead. After we left each other, I came home and found a message from her. I called your office line and left a message. I checked her apartment. It looked like someone had done a snatch and grab from her bedroom. I drove to the office and found out some information on her employment before I headed back home. I heard about your car accident while I was getting a burger and knew something was not right. By the time I got home, there were teams at both ends of my block. I have been on the run since. No one knows I'm here either."

"But how did you know where I was?" Jeff asked.

"My job is a little different than yours, but we're both on the same team, trust me. I went through some notes of Maria's work and did a little research myself. By the time I was done, I believed the CIA's fingerprints were all over her disappearance. I have knowledge of certain aspects of their job, some of their methods, and locations where people go. It was a guess that they had taken Maria to "the Point". Imagine my surprise when I came downstairs and found you. I couldn't very well leave you."

"Well, I'm glad you didn't. You are going to need me to keep you out of prison. Some of those people died."

"I'm not concerned with that now. I was until they chased after us and tried to kill us. Until they killed my friend who was helping us."

"I'm sorry about your friend. If he or she had a family, maybe the Bureau can help. Where do you think Maria is? Do you think she is even alive at this point? Look, Wilson, we are going to need some help on this. I am not concerned about the Bureau. They loath the CIA. Let me reach out to them."

"I'm not going to keep you here, Jeff. If you are ready to roll tomorrow, I will truck you out to a roadside and you are on your own. However, you had better make sure the Bureau is around you because these guys can put a story together like no one else. I've seen it before."

"Tomorrow, I'll be ready," he said.

They spent the rest of the morning walking around the house outside discussing Maria. Jeff offered the help of a retired U.S. Marshall, saying he might be willing to join them and get to the bottom of what was going on. They needed help and surely there were some trustworthy agents at headquarters he could call. Wilson did not offer any thoughts. His silence told Jeff he wasn't interested. They came from two different worlds. The FBI was one of laws and courts. Wilson's was simply who carried the biggest stick.

They ate lunch and he pulled out 2 steaks to thaw for dinner before they sat down with a cold beer to watch FOX News. Wilson asked Jeff if he knew anything about the house that blew up and the guy who was shot in the head.

He looked down at his feet a moment and shook his head side to side slowly before carefully answering.

"Was that your work or their work?"

"That was my house. Robbie was a friend of mine. He took my place. I didn't know he was going to, but he saved my life. I will find who did that and I will find who gave the order to them. Whoever did that will not see Court," he added.

"Can I ask you, Wilson, is that something separately related to you or is that related to Maria too?"

"It's Maria."

"Do you think Maria's disappearance and my abduction are really related to 9/11?"

Wilson measured his words carefully.

"Jeff, I don't involve myself in other agency's events. I do not know much about 9/11 except what I have read. Maria found something related to it; something that she believed was huge. She may have gotten carried away and put a premise out there that upset people in certain areas. You would know better than I would. I have no idea what questions you were asked."

"I was groggy most of the time going in and out of consciousness. They electrocuted me. They water boarded me. They injected me around the clock with something. They wanted to know what Judge Henderson told me. They wanted to know if Maria had spoken to me. They wanted to know how long we had been friends, you and I. They asked me where you were hiding. And, they wanted to know my knowledge of 9/11. Why would they ask me that? I think these were American agents. Speaking of that, where do you work Wilson? Whom do you work for that you think is going to cover all this up? This is a mess."

"Jeff, I can't tell you who I work for. I can tell you we are the same friends we have always been. I will go after those that went after you, trust me. I do not have any more of the puzzle than you do. I wish I did, but I do not. I am not sure that even matters to me. Now, thanks to "the Point", I can't go back to my office either until this is over."

Wilson was frustrated and needed to let it go. He got up and prepared the steaks. It had been awhile since he made his marinade and he hoped cooking would give him a measure of escape. He found the barbecue sauce, soy sauce, mustard, steak sauce, Worcestershire, a little garlic, some red wine, and set them to soak. He joked with Jeff that last meals should be the best. A couple potatoes were set to bake and he poured some whiskey for both of them.

"Grab your drink Jeff and bring it outside. I'll tell you a story about a guy I met that you would like."

They sat down and Wilson told him about Gus and how they met. He did not tell him any NSA stories or about the property secrets – or about Prince. However, the story was long enough that darkness fell and they had refilled their drinks three times. By the time he grilled the steaks and set the potatoes out, both of them were famished.

They ate in silence, both of them in their own thoughts.

When Jeff pushed himself away from the table, he pronounced it the best meal ever. This time, Wilson agreed. No one made a meaner steak than he did; at least no one here now.

Jeff gave out a big yawn and said he could sleep a week. Wilson told him he would clean up, so go ahead, and go to bed. There was no one to send on patrol. After the kitchen was spotless, he locked the door and sadly walked down the hall to bed. The day's reminder came back to him.

In the morning they both agreed it was time to leave. He told Jeff he would have to blindfold him. This home was all the safety net he had left in the world and he didn't want anyone to know how to find him. Jeff agreed but asked to use a phone first. Wilson proposed a compromise with him. He told him he would call the Bureau on his behalf within minutes of his release. Jeff agreed and gave him the name and number of a female agent. It was one person Jeff said he could trust for sure.

They went outside and Wilson covered Jeff's head with a pillowcase. He picked up his quick bag, grabbed Jeff's elbow to guide him and they began to walk.

"Really? Really," he said. "I have to walk like this."

Wilson held onto him and after a struggle of stops and starts, they finally reached the pump. He made Jeff promise he would leave the case on until Wilson said to take it off. He agreed. Wilson twisted the pump and soon the Jeep appeared. He put Jeff in the passenger seat and buckled him in. Once the navigational screen was powered up, they were on their way. If the people at the ranch noticed anything odd when they passed by the barn, no one gave notice. Wilson drove out and onto the highway, driving in the opposite direction of Gus' town. It would not do to have the FBI crawling all over it. It soon became apparent he could not go much farther without someone noticing a rider with a pillowcase over their heads and calling the local Sheriff.

Wilson told Jeff to keep his eyes closed and substituted dark sunglasses for the pillowcase. He realized it was taking a chance but he trusted Jeff at his word. They passed several gas stations and a couple small towns before he picked Toms Brook, a town of about 200 people, to leave him in. Jeff would be safe there. He pulled in front of Bakers Store, one of the local grocery stores.

"Alright my friend. Open your eyes. You are on your own. I will make the call. I would not contact anyone else until your agent gets here. Who knows who is on what team, Jeff."

"I don't know how I can repay you Mike," he said. They shook hands and he closed the Jeep's door and walked inside.

When he was out of sight, Wilson pulled out a trac phone and made the call as promised. He also moved down the highway about a half-mile and drove off the road into the tree line. He took out his bag and assembled the sniper rifle to keep an eye on Jeff. Ninety minutes later a dark gray government sedan drive up. A female exited and walked into the store. She and Jeff came out together and they both were pretty animated. He must be sharing his story. He was on his own now. Wilson could do nothing more for him.

He disassembled his rifle, packed it, and loaded up. He decided to drive into Gus' town and arrange to pick up Prince. He wanted to bury him on Gus' property. It was his home after all. He was probably the most hated man right now. He drove to the store where Penny would be working. It was time to face the music. He climbed out of the Jeep and went inside.

Doc was sitting around the stove talking and a hush fell over everyone as Wilson approached. Obviously, he was persona non grata. Wilson said hello and something pressed against his leg. He looked down to find Prince. He had a shaved area about ten inches wide on the outside and inside of his right shoulder. There was Frankenstein stitching in a circle around that. Two tiny areas were puckered and also had stiches. None of this seemed to bother him. Wilson kneeled down and buried his face into Prince's. Prince growled, but didn't move. Wilson felt his cheeks streak with tears and wiped them before standing up.

Doc walked across the room and said, "I couldn't give up on him. After you left, I wanted to see for myself what happened to him. When I was looking through my Vet refrigerator, I found this vial of serum Gus had brought me. I'm not sure what's in it besides Yellow flower, E Zhu, and horse tail powder but he told me if a kick was needed for an animal that was hurt badly, I had nothing to lose by trying this. It's been in the refrigerator since. I gave Prince a huge dose and got a better pulse right afterwards. I was afraid to give him any anesthesia so Penny helped me shave him and I found two gunshots. I cut him open and he didn't move much, but then again he was pretty weak. I tried to be as gentle as I could. Both bullets had hit bone; hit his shoulder as a matter of fact, and one deflected. It wasn't inside him. The other one was lodged in the shoulder blade. I removed it and a small bone chip. By the time I sewed him back up, his pulse had dropped again and was barely discernible.

Penny spent the night with him and in the morning, he was gone. She thought he had died and I had taken him away. We called him but he never came. We wondered if maybe you came and got him.

This morning a couple people said, they saw him limping, but that damn animal is like a ghost. You see him, and then you don't. We weren't certain."

Wilson shook Doc's hand and thanked him. Penny looked at him and winked.

"I'm sorry for letting Prince get hurt," Wilson said. "He saved my life. Gus entrusted me with him and I will do better. I promise."

Penny asked, "Will you stay for lunch? Just about everyone is coming. The town heard the news last night and went to bed, some angry, some upset to the point of tears. We all felt bad.

Prince's recovery was like a Christmas morning. It has been nothing short of a miracle. We have been yakking about it since dawn."

"Perhaps I shouldn't. I am the one that caused the wave of emotions. There might be some folks here that cannot forget that. I don't want to ruin your celebration."

"You might be right," she laughed, "But people need to meet you and make their own judgment. You are kind of our Gus junior. Besides, I am not sure Doc is ready for you to take Prince back, so a little ass-kissing might be in order, *Mr.* Wilson." She tossed her hair and went back behind the counter.

Penny asked Doc to introduce him around again when they got to the barbecue. Wilson offered to buy the groceries saying he was left a small sum recently and couldn't think of a more worthy event. Doc was delighted with that. He and others walked around the store picking items from a list his wife had made earlier. Wilson walked out and grabbed some cash from his bag.

He squared up with Penny and pocketed the rest.

"What can I do to pay Doc Rhinehart back?"

"Pay the vet bill," she said.

She locked the door and asked for a ride over to the barbecue. There were several people there he had not met. Doc set up the barbecue and got it going. His wife Mae gave Wilson a hug and whispered in his ear to let God handle all his worries and just have fun day today. She and Penny rolled up their sleeves along with some of the other people and began making side dishes.

Wilson decided to introduce himself to those he had not met. He tried to couch questions without appearing too nosy or interrogating them as he moved from table to table to visit. All eyes seemed on him one time or another. Initially their responses were guarded and no one talked about Gus in any depth or professed to have any knowledge of his background. Each and everyone however spoke praises of him saying he had been a really good friend to all of them through the years. They were clearly loyal to him.

As the afternoon wore on, Wilson learned who was related to who, how long each one had lived here and the bonds they had made. It also was pointed out just how much they loved Prince. He was their dog too. He sensed some of the people were conflicted about what had happened to Prince when he was in Wilson's care. Their facial expressions and tones conveyed they blamed him.

He helped clean up while Penny bundled food. Mae was busy sending leftovers home with everyone while he finished bringing in dishes. People folded up tables and chairs, gave generous hugs to each other, and said good-by to Wison.

After nearly an hour, Mae and Penny sat down on the front porch with some iced tea. Doc and Wilson grabbed a couple

Bud Lights. Doc let him settle the vet bill. It wasn't cheap. The four of them chatted about the dinner. Wilson decided it was time to bring up Prince's leaving.

"So, Doc, what's your prognosis on Prince? Does he need to stay here for a few more days or a week? Or can he come home?"

His question was met by a pregnant silence.

Mae spoke first.

"Harold, you need to be Christian about this. You do not make the rules in life. I like Mike and I think he would give his life for Prince. You can't ask for more than that."

Wilson waited.

"Mae, when I rescued that little fella from that wolf den, I wasn't sure if it was the right thing to do. He was one of a kind, and even in his first few months, he displayed a fierce loyalty. I gave him to Gus knowing Gus would protect him and he would protect Gus. Prince has a need to be very loyal to one person. I do not know where Gus went or why Prince made the transition to Mike here. I know Prince made it. They both have. I can see it. Nonetheless, I felt a feeling I had not felt in years when I thought he was dead. I remember when we buried our first-born. All these thoughts came flooding back. Damn dog made me cry."

Mae said, "You still haven't answered Mike's question."

Doc answered, "Prince will leave when he's ready. I say that because I do not know that anyone actually 'owns' him or ever will. Gus always felt the same way, as if Prince was more of an enigma. He takes commands well; I know Gus trained him to do many things but if Prince did not want to do something, he wouldn't. I think he looks like an abnormal German shepherd because that is what people want to see. I see a wolf. He is very independent, he knows how to hunt, he is not very trusting, and he moves like a ghost, especially at night. He loves the night. In fact, none of us knows where he goes to at night.

Listen to me go on and on. He is ready to leave. If I said no, he'd probably walk all the way back anyway."

Penny squeezed Wilson's hand. He felt good again. He had not seen Prince in about an hour, but he was not going to leave without him.

"Anything I need to do special for him?" he asked the doc.

"Make sure he gets plenty of rest and you keep the sutured areas clean. I do not envy you that part. He's not going to be a good patient."

"Well then, time for me to get moving."

"One more thing," Doc said, "Could you bring him back in a little while to visit? I'd be obliged."

Wilson gave him his word that he would and walked over to the Jeep. He pulled out the small digital device from his bag away from their view. He tapped the screen twice and put it away. He waved goodbye and started the Jeep. Prince appeared out of nowhere on the porch in front of Doc. He stood up on his hind legs, pushed his head into Doc's for a long moment, and then jumped down. Wilson set his bag on the ground with the passenger door open. Prince trotted over and used the bag like a step to jump inside.

They headed back to Gus' place. It was a beautiful day. They got back to the platform and he told Prince to stay while he turned the pump. He jumped back in and they rode down together. Judging by Prince's reaction, Wilson suspected he had done this many times before. He waited until the ceiling was in place, grabbed his bag and set it on the ground before opening the passenger door. Prince stepped out slowly. Wilson hoisted his bag and walked off with Prince following behind him.

By the time they reached the door, his limp was very noticeable. Wilson did the trick with the T-bar and the wall moved. They went inside and after a few minutes, the wall closed. He went to the refrigerator and got the dual syringes containing the liquid bandage. There were plenty left. Upstairs he did a cursory check of the house confirming no one had been inside. The front door had not opened from when he left this morning with Jeff according to the thread set on the sill. Prince soon joined him, lying on the floor in front of Gus' chair. When Wilson approached him with the liquid bandage in hand, Prince growled. Wilson knelt down and Prince flashed his teeth as a warning.

Wilson didn't care. This was going to help him and he was counting on Prince to trust him. Prince didn't move so he applied the liquid bandage to the sutured areas. He would heal faster and now they did not have to worry about infection.

He made sure chow was out and there was fresh water in the bowls for Prince before he grabbed a beer and sat down in Gus' chair to do some thinking.

Prince would need a couple weeks before being 100% was his guess. He was not going wait two weeks. He would need to report in soon and had a lot of explaining to do. Maybe he could take Prince back to Doc's when he was ready to go. They would enjoy the time together and it would be one less thing to be concerned about.

Tomorrow he would contact Jeff. Based on what was happening with Jeff and the exchange between the Bureau and the CIA, Wilson would know his next step and in what direction politically this was going. The agencies would need people to blame and people to terminate. A chain of events like that set other events in motion. It accelerated some and it changed others. If they had not killed Maria yet, they certainly could not do it now. She would be moved again. When they transferred her, Wilson would know.

He watched a little TV and into the evening found himself nodding off. He got up and Prince was gone. His dog chow was eaten and his water gone, too. That was a good sign. Wilson refilled the water dish, locked up and went down the hall to bed.

* * *

The next morning he woke up to bright sunlight and realized he had not pulled down any shades last night. Prince was lying on the floor in the hallway. He stepped over him and went in to shave and shower. Most of his clothes needed washing so he began doing laundry next.

He put on a pot of coffee and filled Prince's dish with dog chow. His water was nearly empty and he gave him another fresh bowl. Prince probably had a little fever which was another reason to go stay with Doc for a while. While waiting for the last load to dry, he pulled out a trac phone and called the FBI female agent's phone number from the day before. He told her he was the driver who brought her friend back and asked if she would hand him her phone.

"We really would like to help you find your son, but you have to understand the Bureau receives over 750,000 missing children reports a year, Mr. Camarada. Do you have an email address that I can send updates to or a website should we get any?" she asked.

"Camarada" was another word in Spanish for friend. He didn't know if someone was listening in or why she was taking such precautions if the Bureau had been informed by Jeff of his kidnapping. She hadn't earned his trust yet either. He told her he would call her back in twenty minutes and disconnected.

He went downstairs and powered up the computer. PASSWORD flashed. He entered the NSA password as he had done previously. The digital timer popped up on screen. He only needed three minutes. He created a drop box that only NSA level V employees could access and signed out before powering off.

Seventeen minutes later, Wilson called her back and gave her the electronic address for the drop-box. If anyone were tracking her it would tell them they are communicating with someone inside the NSA. That should be enough to slow them down, if not cause them major concern.

He waited and powered up the computer, then logged back in. There was a message in the drop box: "Need to meet. See you at the store, 7 PM tonight."

He signed out and powered off. He had no idea what her plan was, but he had one. He sat there and waited twenty minutes before logging back on.

The clock started and he used the NSA power to once again log into "Sally Sue" remotely. He found the file Maria had copied and began to read.

"Virtually all of the structural steel from the Twin Towers and Building 7 was removed and destroyed prior to forensic analysis. FEMA's volunteer investigators did manage to perform 'limited metallurgical examination' of some of the steel before it was recycled. This showed that the microstructural analysis revealed inter-granular (Swiss cheese-like) melting due to a liquid that contained a high content of sulfur, iron, and oxygen – not jet fuel, not kerosene.

Two renowned science professors examined this small bit of evidence and concurred saying it was 'arson' – not jet fuel that turned steel into Swiss cheese and into this type of dust never seen before. One of those was Steven Jones with twenty years of experience in the field of physics."

There was too much and it was too technical for the time Wilson had. Randomly, he scanned the next pages and learned that all but one of the Arabs the CIA identified by name as the hijackers surfaced alive in other countries the very next week. There was nothing logical or acceptable about this. He needed to walk away from it and the sooner the better. He logged out and powered off.

He found Prince upstairs and talked to him similar to how one might talk to a child. He explained he had to take him back to Doc's for a couple weeks, but he would be coming back. He armed up and motioned Prince downstairs. Wilson had never opened up the wall from inside before and he did not have a lot of time to locate the trigger. He stood in front of it and tried to motion what he needed Prince to do. Wilson waved at it; he tugged at an imaginary handle. He walked into the wall marching forward. After a several minutes, he just said aloud, "Prince open the door."

He should have started with that command. Prince walked over to the wall that led to the tunnel and pushed a light switch up with his nose. The floor began to slide and they were in. Too simple, he thought. He told Prince to lie on the cart but Prince refused. They walked the distance to the Jeep and Wilson set his bag down for him to use as a step. Wilson had never left this way, but he knew that turning off the Jeep trigged the ceiling to close so he started it up. The platform began to move and the ceiling opened up, trading places. Once they were above ground, Wilson powered on the navigational screen and they headed out. He unlocked and locked the chain across the National Forest road they had come down. They crossed the ranch and soon arrived at the town Gus had built. He found the Doc's house and Mae answered the door.

"Is Doc around?" Wilson asked.

"Oh dear is it Prince? Is he worse?"

"No, he's fine. I have to leave for a few days unexpectedly and I want to leave Prince here so I'll know he's okay while I am gone."

"Doc is taking a nap, but have Prince come in and I'll wake him up."

Wilson got Prince out and walked him inside. Doc was just putting on his shoes. "How long will you be, son?"

"I have no idea. I'll get back as soon as I can but it will probably be about two weeks. Is that okay?"

They looked at each other and he could tell Doc was excited.

"You bet, Mike. We will take good care of him. What's that plastic coat on his wounds?"

"Leave it. Please. It is a military grade liquid bandage. He will heal quicker."

Wilson turned to Prince and knelt down. He told him to stay here and take care of Mae and Doc. He walked out the door and did not look back.

He had an idea of the direction to Toms Brook, but the navigation system made quick work of it. The front of the store looked normal as he passed by. It was about 5 PM when he moved down the road and drove off into the tree line to hide the Jeep. The closest pine tree had a great branch to sit in.

He assembled his sniper rifle, chambered a round, and began the wait. He was good at waiting but, didn't to do it long. A black van with tinted windows pulled up on one side of the store and two teams got out. They took up positions on both sides. Surprise, surprise.

He disassembled his rifle, packed up and drove the Jeep through the trees parallel to the road. When he got about a mile past Bakers store, Wilson pulled the Jeep out into the two-lane road, blocking most of one lane and partially the other. He turned on the flashers and kneeled down as if he were looking for something. He waited. He had squatted there for about a half-hour when a vehicle approached. It was a farm truck so he turned off the flashers and waved at the driver as he passed by, giving him the universal thumbs-up sign.

After it was out of sight, he set the Jeep back in place, flashers on, and had just knelt down when over his shoulder he saw government Ford coming. He could hear it slow down. It stopped and he heard the door open and light footsteps approaching.

"You're blocking the road. Can I help you or call someone for you," she asked.

Wilson pointed his cocked .45 at her face. "Yes, how about calling Jeff? What do you think? Will he pick up?"

He put her down, removed two weapons, taped her mouth and put her in plastic cuffs. He stuffed her in the trunk and moved her car to the side of the road. She had country-western music playing. It was tempting for him to go back and kill every one they had sent to the store. However, he thought of something different. If their "agent" disappeared, they wouldn't know how far she had gotten nor who took her. Let them chew on that for a while. He positioned the Jeep just off to the side of the road.

He started the Ford and drove it off the main road and up into the tree line carefully, so it didn't leave tracks. Luckily, it hadn't rained in sometime and the ground was hard. He took a branch and swept some areas before jogging back to the Jeep. He circled off-road in the Jeep and took the long way back to the Ford. This way if someone saw the tracks it would look like a four-wheeler was out driving.

Once he got back to the Ford, he opened the trunk. He checked the woman's pockets and removed everything that was not sewn in. He did not mean to be indelicate, but he unbuttoned her shirt and cut her bra off. He did not have time to admire her. Nothing was hidden there. She was pissed, but this was purely to protect his location. Underwired bras were very conducive to signals. He did not know who made hers; and he sure as hell didn't know who she worked for. He buttoned her shirt back up and began to remove her skirt. This time she fought harder and kicked so he had to put her in a sleeper hold until she went limp. He removed her skirt, pulled her nylons down and cut her panties off. Nothing there either. He pulled her nylons back up and put her skirt back on. She was placed in the back seat of the Jeep and he taped her feet and hands to the seat frame. He covered her with a thin yellow accident blanket from the first aid box.

Her bra and panties were checked thoroughly and he found nothing extraordinary. He went through her purse and did find a listening device inside her cell phone. This type of device allowed for listening whether the phone was on or off. He was hoping they did not hear the road stop conversation. He thought back and they had not been close enough to it that it could be heard over her country music. He removed his Marine K-bar knife from his bag and took the phone apart, smashing it on the bumper. He removed the battery and pried off the battery cables so there would be no power to the car. He destroyed her purse and everything else by dismantling or slashing it. It was time to go. This had taken seven minutes from the time she stopped. He was not happy with losing so much time.

He powered up the navigational screen and put the Jeep in low, crawling his way through the surrounding hills back into the National Forest. It was dark by the time they arrived at the locked chain. He passed through, relocked it, and headed directly for home. His passenger had wakened and he sensed letting her out of the cuffs and tape would be like letting a wild cat out of a gunnysack.

He wasted no time when driving onto the platform. He turned the pump and jumped back on as the Jeep headed underground. Once the ceiling locked in place, he had made his decision. She was staying right here. He was not taking her into the house. She could not be heard yelling and if he took the keys, she was not leaving. There was a small bathroom in the corner with a sink and running water. It had a toilet. She would be fine for a couple days if necessary. He had noticed a floor to ceiling sliding door that had a drop-latch lock on the farwall so he walked over and opened it. It took some muscle to budge it along sideways. Inside was a cot. Maybe Gus stayed here sometimes. He cut the woman loose and lifted her out of the Jeep. She struggled but he sensed she was scared. He set her on the cot, removed her tape, then the plastic cuffs.

He stepped back and waited for her to speak. She covered her chest with her arms. Tears welled up in her eyes.

"I am a Federal Agent. The entire Bureau of the FBI will be looking for me. If you let me go, I will testify you did not hurt me. LET – ME – GO – NOW!"

Wilson spoke softly and pointed with the K-bar to the bathroom. He told her she had four minutes to use the toilet and then he was locking her up for the night. She did not move. He told her one minute had just gone by.

She stood up, straightened her clothes and walked over to the bathroom closing the door with as much dignity as she could muster. A few minutes later she came out and tears were running down her face. She stopped in mid-stride. He told her she could do this the easy way or the hard way, but she had to get inside the room with the cot now. She took a deep breath and walked past him towards the cot. As she passed, she dropped and did a kicking sweep with her feet. He saw it coming and stepped out of range. She landed as if she was a ballerina, and stood up. Hatred rolled off her face.

He stepped out and with quite an effort, closed the door. He dropped the latch in place and made sure there was no way to lift it from her location. He then took the Jeep keys and his bag with him before he walked down the tunnel.

At the end, he worked the T-bar and got inside. Once the floor moved and the wall closed up, Wilson went upstairs to shower. He had been ordered to kill people, had killed people because they needed killing, and he had extracted information from people. He was not a pervert or a rapist. No matter how much soap he used, he did not feel clean after this last move. He would let her think until morning. She needed to believe this was serious. He doubted anything like this had ever happened to her and working for the Bureau, she would have never prepared for it. It would be all psychological from here on out.

What happened? Did she deliver Jeff? Did they just pick him up, again? Were they monitoring Bureau calls? He had not been on the trac that long when he spoke with her and he never mentioned Jeff by name. He replayed his rescue in his mind. There was no way Jeff had been role-playing. He and Jeff were on the same team.

He was tired and lay on top of the bed with his .45 nearby. He didn't have Prince so he wasn't feeling very secure about closing his eyes.

Taking her would cause a firestorm from two sides. She was right that the FBI would light up like a switchboard within one to two days. He also knew the other side would increase the manpower into the area after she failed to arrive in Toms Brook. He needed to prevent that. If he let that continue long enough, enough people looking from either or both teams would discover Gus' town. Funny, he never asked if it had a name, but it was up to him to prevent that happening. He needed to make his presence known elsewhere within thirty-six to forty-eight hours. Tick-tock.

The sun woke him up and he shaved and dressed. Putting the .45 at the small of his back, he rummaged through the drawers in Gus' room. Under the closet was a long drawer with women's clothes and other stuff. There was a full make-up kit, wigs, and various women's clothing including shoes. Most of it was new. He grabbed a sleeveless tee. His remaining choices were a folded business suit, a flowery sundress, a high-waisted skirt of some sorts and a pair slacks. He opted for the slacks and did not care how well they fit. She probably was not going to change anyway. There was no underwear. He went back to his room and grabbed a clean pair of briefs.

Wilson made breakfast, but it did not set well. Something was not right. He had missed something. He put an egg and some bacon on a plate with a fork and grabbed the pile of clothing. Downstairs, he flipped the light switch and when the wall moved, he walked into the tunnel. The wall closed behind him.

He set things on the Jeep's hood and opened the door about ten inches. She was not on or near the cot, which meant she was waiting on the other side of the door.

"Look, Agent. You need to go sit down on the cot. When I see you on the cot, I will bring you breakfast. It is up to you. I can close the door and we can try this again tomorrow."

She never moved so he started to push the door closed.

"Okay, okay," she said.

He opened it ten inches again and he could see she was sitting on the cot. He opened ithe door all the way and told her to stay seated. He brought her breakfast with a fork and set everything on the floor about four feet away.

"Unless you are really good in hand-to-hand combat with a fork, don't even think of using it on me."

She eyed the food warily, and then began to eat. He moved back to the Jeep's bumper and waited until she was finished. He told her to set the plate and fork back where he had placed it. She did so and sat back down.

He removed the plate, put the fork in his back pocket, and set the clean clothing down before stepping back. He told her she might want to change out of her suit. She put her hands on her hips and glared.

"Take the clothes and go into the bathroom and change," he said.

"Where's my bra?" she asked looking through the clothing.

"It's gone. I had to make sure you weren't wired."

"What the hell are you talking about?" she demanded.

"Go change and we'll have that conversation."

"I want my bra."

"Here's your choice. You can either go change and we'll have a discussion when you get back or I put you back behind the door and we'll try it again tomorrow."

She turned in anger and went into the bathroom. When she came back, she tossed the briefs at him and said, "I'm not wearing your underwear to give you some sort of thrill."

The defiance and the pent up anger boiled over and she came at him with every bit of her training and a little more. Her flurry of punches bloodied his nose. He was surprised how quick she was with her fists. She followed this with a sweep kick to bring him down, but Wilson was ready for this and grabbed her foot. He brought it up and over putting her down on the floor harder than he wanted to. The back of her head hit with a sickening thud. He stood up and moved away tasting the blood from his nose running down his throat. He felt his nose and was relieved she had not broken it. He put pressure on his nose using his fingers.

She slowly sat up and grabbed the back of her head. He could not see her face, but knew she would have a headache for a day or two. He just hoped she had not cracked her skull.

"Dammit, dammit," she said. "Do you feel tough beating up a woman?"

"First you came at me and punched me in the nose. We could have just talked. You wanted to fight. You probably wanted to kill me. I couldn't let you do that."

She attempted to get up and he saw her eyes roll back into her head as she fell backward and passed out.

It was then he noticed her tee had pulled up exposing one breast and most of the other. He pulled it down.

Head injuries can be very deceiving; most of the time they can be dangerous. He had heard her head hit and was familiar with that sound. He did not want her to die – not yet. There was only one thing to do. Doc. He could either bring him here or take her to him. If he took her to Doc, the whole town might pay the consequences later.

He laid her on the cot, closed and latched the door, and removed the Jeep keys from his pocket. He jumped in the Jeep and started it. The pad moved and he rotated up. Putting the Jeep in gear, Wilson drove off the platform. He turned the pump, disguising the pad as the corn field moved over it. He powered up the navigational screen and headed out. There was no time to waste.

After a while, he pulled up to the front of Doc's house. He knocked twice and Mae answered the door.

"I need Doc's help. I have an injured friend."

She motioned Wilson in and hurried to the back room. Doc came out carrying his bag.

"Hey there, Mike. What has happened to your friend? Mae told me it was urgent."

"There's no time, Doc. I will tell you on the way. I need you to go with me. Mae, I will bring him back safely. I promise."

Thjey climbed into the Jeep and Wilson drove to the edge of town. He stopped and looked over.

"Doc, have you ever been to Gus' farmhouse?"

"I'm the only one from town that has son. I do not know how to get there because he always asked me to keep my eyes closed. He said if anyone ever came to town looking for him, I could honestly say I didn't know the way."

"Well Doc, close your eyes because that's where we're headed."

"Is it Gus?" he asked.

I put the Jeep in gear and accelerated.

"No, it's a young gal that's in my custody. We had a small fight and I took her down too hard. She hit her head."

"I won't ask you what you do," Doc said. "I made a leap of faith long time ago that Gus was on the right side of the law. I have to do the same with you since you are his guest and all. Is she a bad person?"

"I really am not sure. She has FBI credentials and she claims to be one of their agents. I was going to talk with her this morning when she lashed out at me."

"But you're not sure if she is or isn't, right? I mean if she is, am I going to be in any trouble treating her?"

"My boss can fix just about anything if I'm wrong. I need you to make sure she's not going to die and I'll run you back to Mae."

"How well do you know Gus? I mean, how long have you known him?" Doc asked.

Wilson did not reply.

Doc sighed and said, "Years ago, about eighteen, to be exact, I had a practice in the midwest. Ohio. Mae and I had raised our kids and were looking to move. I put my practice up for sale hoping someone would buy it. I was only fifty-five years old, but I had a large number of patients. Whatever I got for that was going to be our retirement. Mae had saved over the years too. Then Gus came along. I got a phone call on a Sunday afternoon. This man asked if I was still interested in selling my practice saying he had a proposition for me. I assured him I was and invited him for supper. You see, I didn't want just anyone treating my patients. I wanted to be sure I left them in good hands.

"He was affable enough. We discussed his training and he produced papers from a briefcase showing he had done his internship at Walter Reed Medical Center. He was older than I was.

Mae insisted we continue our discussion over supper. By the time we finished, he made his proposition to us. Gus asked if we would be amenable to retiring to Virginia. That did not set well with Mae and she said she did not think so. He only smiled and continued with his offer.

"He had built a town. We could walk around it and pick our house. He'd pay the utilities. We had to pay for our gas and groceries. He did not expect us to use our retirement for that though.

"He would pay me a salary to be the town physician. Course I told him, aside from the money, then I would not be retired, now would I?

"Gus assured me that my services would be minimal. The hospital in the area was going to be receiving a generous donation and they would handle anything serious or long-term. Well, you can imagine this sounded a bit bizaar, to Mae and me. We are just simple people. Why would some stranger want to do this? In addition, who owned a town?

"Before Gus left that night, he assured me if at any time we were not comfortable, he would pay to move us back to Ohio or wherever we wanted to go. He left his card on the table and left. He also assured me he would find someone to purchase and take over my existing practice. He also promised I would be given final approval.

"Neither one of us slept much that night. We talked about it for days. I told Mae we had nothing to lose by checking his town out. Maybe we would like it. It was way outside our comfort zone, but there was something about Gus I liked.

"We accepted his offer. We have been very happy, we met new people and I feel very good that if I were to pass before Mae, she would have a home the rest of her life.

"Everyone in town has their own Gus story. We have no crime. We come and go as we please. We never swore an oath but I suspect Gus chose like-minded people."

They arrived at the pump house. Wilson asked Gus to continue to keep his eyes closed. Wilson jumped off, pushed the pump, and jumped back on the Jeep driving it forward when the pad surfaced. Once it lowered completely and the ceiling was in place, he turned the ignition off.

"Now you can open your eyes. Come with me."

Wilson unlatched and pushed open the tall door. Gus walked inside and knelt down over Wilson's prisoner. He removed his stethoscope and blood pressure cuff from his bag. After an examination, he stood up with a sigh.

"Mike, I don't know what's going on or what's in play here as I said earlier. This young lady is comatose. I cannot tell if she has a skull fracture or not without a CAT-scan. I do not know if she is going to make it. She needs to be hospitalized."

"We can't do that Doc; not this time. She has answers that I need. If she goes into a hospital, I will not get them. The Bureau or worse will come and believe me, they will learn about all of us. I can't let that happen."

"Mike, if you don't move this gal pretty soon, she might die. I cannot do her any good here. I took an oath as a physician."

Wilson gave this some thought. If she died, he was no further behind. He would have to pick up where he last saw Jeff and move forward. It would have to start with her anyway. It would just be quicker if she told him.

On the other hand, if she were an FBI agent, and an honest one, he would have killed someone that did not deserve it. He liked her. There, he admitted it, at least to himself. She had grit. She reminded him of Annie.

"Doc, if you take her to the hospital, can you get her admitted under any name? Can you be sure she does not talk to the staff? They would end up calling the FBI. I need maybe twenty to twenty-five minutes with her if she wakes up."

"I'll do my best. I have only dealt with my contact at Page Memorial that Gus set up one time. It was when Penny had ovarian cancer. I know we will have a private room and assigned nurses. She will not be in general admitting, but it will not be a prison ward either. They only have twenty-five beds."

"All right, let's do it."

They placed her in the Jeep. Doc climbed in and took her head into his lap.

"I hate to ask this, Doc …"

"Yeah, I know, close my eyes." He did.

He brought the Jeep up to the surface and headed back to Gus' town as soon as the pad dropped. It was almost noon. They made the transfer to the back of Mae's station wagon. Mae came out and climbed into the front passenger seat of her car without saying a word.

"Doc, what about Prince? Where is he?"

"You know him. He comes and goes. He is doing better, but he needs to stay longer, Mike. It's been a busy week."

"All right, let me give you a cell phone. Put this SIM chip in the backside like this and turn it on when you have some news. Keep your call brief. Contrary to the movies, most cell phones can't be traced in less than twenty minutes, but people can listen. On – then off and remove the SIM chip. Press the number one button and it will dial me."

Wilson handed him the phone and watched him drive off. He turned his head and looked around at the town. His own town; practically his own hospital, had to cost Gus millions of dollars, not to mention his property and the ranch on the other side of the National Forest. He was sure he owned that too. Either Gus was a lottery winner, had quite a 401-K, or an even better pension – or, Gus *was* the government. He needed to get moving.

He arrived back at the pad and dropped below ground. Seeing the empty cot reminded him how badly things had gone. He was not one to wait. He picked up her clothing from the bathroom and walked down the tunnel. He worked the push-pull sequence and entered the downstairs.

Her credentials said her name was Jill Carlson. There had not been any point going on line earlier when he had her. Now, her name was all there was. He set her clothes down and powered up the computer before entering the password. The countdown began once more. The database he wanted into this time was at Quantico. He wanted to look at training files for Jill Carlson. He was unable to get in without going through NSA, so he did. It created a tracking risk should she die.

Jill Carlson was born in Battle Creek, Michigan, and had the right age, weight and height. Her background check had a photo to match. There was nothing remarkable about her except she had a photographic memory. Her mentor suggested the Bureau explore that trait further. Swell. This meant she could work with a sketch artist and they'd have a photo of Wilson in no time.

While he was in, he thought to enter Maria Styletti's name again. He had flagged it earlier for any inquiries. There was no activity. He was going to enter Jeff's name but he was running out of time and logged out. He powered it off.

He ran upstairs and pulled out another trac phone activating it for fifteen minutes. Every fifteen minutes he would power it on, wait fifteen , and power it off. It really was not necessary, but he stayed alive by doing more than he had to. Most of the phone company switching equipment in this country was analog until the mid-1980s. Some remained and it took a lot of wire tracing and switch-work to track a number. The majority, including cellular, moved into the digital arena. However, it still was not like one saw in the movies. Tracing worked within minutes if not seconds on the big screen. As he told Doc, real life took about twenty minutes and took much more equipment than any state or local agency had. His concern was eavesdropping. The NSA was very good at listening. Ever since Snowden released information about the abilities of the NSA, the American public – and a few agents like him that were "off-the-grid", were paranoid.

Wilson still was not seeing something. A piece of the puzzle. He pulled out a cold Bud Light, made some spaghetti and sat down to eat. He monitored the phone powering it on and off at intervals, while cleaning up. He needed to check his drop box so he dug through his bag for the smart phone and logged onto Gus' router.

The drop box for Annie was empty. He sent one more message in their code. It was indecipherable to anyone else and said, "Meet me inside my D.C. apartment tomorrow night; now more than ever." Would it be safe? Well, if she came, it would be safe for him – not for others. He logged out and removed his SIM card.

He powered the trac phone on after putting the other SIM card in and waited again. He was rewarded. Doc called.

"Come here. You can talk," and hung up.

Jill must have been alive and alert. Good news. He armed up, set a hair on the front door, and went downstairs.

He managed to locate the hospital in under an hour. Visiting hours were over, but he told the receptionist that Doctor Rhinehart was expecting him. She picked up a phone, buzzed someone and hung up. Whoever it was called her back and she asked Wilson for his name.

"Mike Wilson," he told her.

"Dr. Rhinehart is on the second floor in room twenty-four at the end of the hall. Stairs are to your right and elevators are to your left."

He went to the right and ran up. There was a central desk with one nurse and another doctor talking. They gave him a casual glance as he walked down the hall to room twenty-four.

"Hey doc, how's she doing," he asked.

"Ask her yourself. She's got a bad headache, but she'll live." He stepped out the door saying he would be right outside, reading her chart.

Jill looked up at Wilson, "Why did you abduct me?"

"Jill, there's a lot at stake here and not a lot of time to explain. I am sorry about taking you down and you getting hurt. We have to move past that. You're a federal agent and we are on the same team – I think."

"You think? Jeff told me you were his friend and your name is Mike Wilson."

"Why were those take-down teams at the store you told me to go to?"

"I have no idea what you are talking about," she said. "I never saw anyone on the highway in front or behind me until I stopped to help you."

"How did they know to go to Toms Brook – and to that specific grocery store?"

"Maybe when I signed out the Bureau car?"

"Tell me about that," he said.

"I'm not senior enough to warrant a take-home car. I take the metro to work and checkout a motor pool car when I need one. I am so used to writing the location I am going to; I did not think not to write that one down. I'm sorry."

"Where's Jeff now?"

"I left him at the house where I am staying for the summer. I housesit when I can and mooch off folks in-between. D.C. is too expensive for a beginning Agent's salary. Hand me that pad and pencil and I'll write the address down for you."

"Does the Bureau know he is alive?"

"No."

"What about you? What kind of cover story did you give?"

"Doctor Rhinehart was reluctant but he let me call in as long as I let him listen. I told our receptionist I had some female problems and needed a couple days. I can be out for three to five days before I need to make contact or go back in."

"Good. If they release you, will you go with Doc and stay at his house, please?"

"I will on one condition."

"What's that?"

"You buy me a new bra."

* * *

The sun did not wake him when it rose the next morning. He slept late. He got up and headed for the bathroom. He had not checked his wound in days so he peeled the bandage off and found it had healed up. It looked great. He hoped Prince's would do the same.

Carefully, Wilson did some stretches and some push-ups, and ran in place for about ten minutes. His mind was clear and he ran through everything while he showered. He packed his quick bag, secured the farmhouse, and placed a hair on the front door. He left a note in Gus' bedroom along with the last bundle of cash. The cash was for the Jeep in case he did not make it back.

Downstairs he powered on the computer one last time. PASSWORD flashed and he logged in to begin the familiar countdown. He looked first in his NSA drop box. There was an encrypted line from a friend at NSA. It welcomed him back, hoped he was well. It told him they had been fending off cyber-attacks and "sophisticated" agency inquiries targeting his login. "Sophisticated" agency inquiries meant someone without Directorate authority was trying to get a line on him.

This was good news. This meant they were desperate and had no idea where he was – yet.

He wanted to move under the cover of darkness, so he sat down to wait for the sun to go down. He found and read a book on Seal Team training that Gus had somehow acquired.

Real men did; other men talked. The afternoon passed. The time came to leave.

Wilson flipped the light switch to enter the tunnel and jogged on up to the Jeep. The Jeep started right up and he moved out into the early evening air. He programmed the nav screen for home and began the journey. When he began passing gas stations, he realized he had not bought gas in some time. It was a good thing he looked. The tank was almost empty so he stopped and filled it up.

About three blocks from the condo, he stopped and parked. He grabbed his quick bag and began walking in the opposite direction. Anytime there was a perceived threat, he knew to do the unexpected first. He had time on his side – they did not. He completed a wide circle. Gradually the circles became smaller until he was on his block. There was a nice stonewall the development had erected some years back and he stopped by it to survey the street. There sat the truck he had abandoned. There was one car parked at the curb ahead of it that was out of place. It had a sticker the size of a base pass on the lower left front of the windshield. No one in this neighborhood drove a large black Chrysler, especially not one with base access.

He armed up. He would take the Chrysler out first and moved up alongside when he noticed both of its occupants. They looked like they were sleeping. They were not. The driver's door window was missing. No glass was on the ground so it must have been lowered deliberately before whatever happened, happened. They were dead. Both had been shot in the temple and set in position. It had not been too long ago either judging from the color of the blood.

He moved on down the street and found a government issued Ford with one more team dead. Carefully, Wilson opened the passenger door. The blood was still seeping. This kill happened in the last eight to ten minutes from his best judgement. They too, had been set into position to warrant minimal curiosity to someone walking or driving by. One was staring straight ahead and the other reading a newspaper. The guy that held a newspaper had been the one to talk was Wilson's guess. His mouth was stuffed with something and each wrist was taped to a thigh. There was a finger-tip taped to the column he had been perusing. Wilson recognized the work.

Whistling with contentment, he grabbed his bag and calmly walked past the other parked cars and door fronts until he reached his condominium building. He jogged up the stairs just as his front door opened.

"Gee, you missed the fun," the familiar voice said.

Annie Chavis was at Hq Engineers with him when they started out in the Corps. They had the same sense of humor, the same laissez-faire attitude about living, and the desire to end a problem without mercy. In short, while they came from different walks of life, they bonded. They became extremely loyal to each other and had been ever since. They endured themselves to the Company Commander, who it turned out, was really in the employment of the CIA. He quietly moved them from Marine Corps Engineer School into an unknown unit of the 2nd.

Annie took assignment after assignment finally leaving one day. Wilson just figured it was by choice and let it be. She did give him a big hug and a kiss saying if he ever needed her, all he had to do was send for her. About that same time, he received a visit one night he suspected he owed to the General. He was interviewed and immediately transferred to "special duty". Since then Wilson reported to one and only one person.

He gave Annie a big hug and his thanks for making his homecoming. She gave him a long and very wet kiss followed by a great smile. As always, she looked terrific. He pulled out a trac phone, called a number and asked that a street cleaner come take care of things. He was told his boss would appreciate his checking in as soon as possible and the conversation ended.

"So here I am big guy. Do you know who those men are?" she asked.

"I was thinking CIA."

"You're right. The one with the newspaper couldn't wait to tell me. They are PSYOP people – scary dudes. When I cut that one guy's finger off, he squirmed a little but he actually smiled too. I was going to hand him something a little lower when he decided he was not that tough. You know me. I can usually make my point rather quickly if I have to. Why are they after you? What the heck did you do now? "

"My neighbor across the hall works on a 9/11 committee at the fed level. She disappeared one night but not before she left me a cryptic message about some files she received from an informant."

Annie raised her eyebrows and her smile disappeared.

"Well, for those boys to put termination orders into effect, she must have really stumbled across something. So, how does that involve you? Didn't you just get back from Europe?"

Wilson explained what had transpired with SAC Tompkins, the camp rescue, and what the "Sally Sue" files told him. He added he still had no idea where Maria was, but doubted she was still alive. He and Tompkins were probably just loose ends.

Annie said, "I never bought into the hijacking story, but like you, I stayed out of it. Someone at the top is going to be pissed about your camp rescue. I can't believe you didn't wait for me. You have to be a hard target now for sure. Can you stop this? You never said who you worked for."

"I can stop it, rather my boss can. He did not authorize my involvement so I do not want to involve him until after we have hit back and hit hard. I want them to pay for coming after me. You know in this town, reputation is everything and I want them to know it cost more than they are willing to spend to come after me, again. There's also a chance that they are still holding onto Maria, but I can't think why."

"Tell you what Michael. Let us see if we cannot get some friends at NSA to listen for your name. What do you think? Let's find out who the one pulling the strings is and take them out."

Wilson told her about the drop box warning and NSA tipping him off to date. They decided that it had to be one of their old teammates, Tracy Hardeback, in algorithms that had seen the hook. She must have been the one that sent the email.

Chavis agreed to make contact with her and see if they could not set up a back-door trace on conversations any time someone spoke about Wilson or Maria Syletti over the air waves.

Chavis asked where they should roost for the night. Wilson suggested the house where Jeff had been stashed. This way, Chavis and Jeff could meet. Chavis pulled out a cell and called NSA to get Tracy's voicemail. She said they needed to do lunch and disconnected knowing Tracy would call her back.

Wilson exited the front and Chavis hopped off the balcony out back. They did a quick sweep. The sun was coming up. The Chrysler and the Ford were going down the road on tow trucks. There was a local police car in front and a black Suburban with privacy windows following. Idyllic life had returned to the neighborhood.

They met up at the house Jill had found to housesit and stash Jeff. It was a mansion on the Potomac. She had failed to mention that. With the mansion came the perk of a gated driveway and perimeter cameras. Wilson said he would go in first so Annie didn't shoot Jeff because he was holding a gun. He came out and gave her the sign to come in.

"Jeff this is Annie Chavis. I trust her more than you, so you don't need to have any concerns about being safe."

"That's a left-handed compliment," Jeff said, "But if I looked like Annie, I would say the same thing."

Annie laughed. They shook hands and sat down to get acquainted. Wilson checked out the house and walked the perimeter inside and outside the block walls. Security was average. They would be safe if they took shifts. He did not like being vulnerable by water, air, and roadway. They had body-bagged several of their agents. The next try might be a mass assault when they finally located them. They needed the FBI to assert its role and halt any CIA activity within the U.S. – specifically, at them. It was time for Jeff to make an appearance.

8. THE TRAP IS SET

Tracy called Annie back on her satellite phone and they agreed to meet in Arlington at Audi Murphy's gravesite. Annie admired Audi Murphy. Wilson asked if she wanted eyes on her and offered to set up. Placing a .22 with a silencer at the small of her back, she declined. She put a second clip in her pocket.

The Old Brogue? Say between 9-10 PM?" She left.

Jeff also agreed it was time to bring in the Bureau. He thought it best to contact his Section Chief. He had known Fred Stevens for fourteen years and believed he was beyond reproach. He was happily married and had two children. They discussed how much information Jeff should give him. Wilson asked Jeff to leave him out of it. Tell him he managed to break free with the help of a recruit at the Point. No one there was going to confirm it happened anyway.

Jeff used a trac phone to call the Bureau and transfer to Stevens. Yes, he was alive. Yes, it was really him. He explained he needed to talk to him secretly today; it was a matter of National Security. Yes, could they meet now if possible? They agreed to meet at the Lincoln Memorial in one hour.

Wilson grabbed his silenced .22. He waited for Jeff to leave and pulled out behind him. Tompkins might spot the tail, but Wilson did not care. He wanted to keep him in sight. He did not worry about Chavis. Annie Chavis took lives. Tompkins investigated lives.

Jeff arrived and found parking about a block away. It took Wilson a little longer before he found a spot on the other side of the pool. Both men approached from different sides because of parking. It turned out to be fortuitous. Jeff bounded up the steps waving to a large man in a brown suit. The man waved back. This had to be Stevens. As they shook hands, Wilson watched a man holding a long coat standing by the Korean War monument pull out what appeared to be a rifle. Wilson ran his way. When he got within his range, Wilson pulled out a silenced .22, draped his jacket over it and fired twice while seemingly bending over to pick up something. The bullets found their mark. The marksman crumbled to the ground as a lady nearby yelled for help. Wilson ran over, appeared to check the fallen man but really removed his wallet. He turned to the lady and said, "Call 911." He told her he was going to find a police officer and quickly left. Within minutes people were crowding to see what had happened followed by U.S. Park and a few D.C. police.

Tompkins and his section Chief were no longer on the stairs. They were gone.

Wilson returned to his car and headed back towards the mansion Jill had secured to house sit. As he entered the neighborhood, he found the street blocked by D.C. police cars. He parked in a driveway where a couple newspapers were piled up and got out of his car. He ambled down the street and saw Jeff walking towards him. They glanced at each other and Wilson joined a group of neighbors talking to one of the officers. This officer enjoyed the attention and was giving out information he shouldn't be. One of the neighbors turned to the others and said he was told an FBI agent had taken his own life because his wife had been unfaithful. He had driven down their street, pulled over, and he shot himself.

Everyone agreed how sad it was and began walking back to their homes. Wilson got back to the Jeep and found Jeff looking at one of the tires. They climbed in and casually drove off.

In about twenty-fiveminutes they were sitting at a table inside "Apehangers" in Maryland. It was a biker bar and agency boys would stand out like a robed terrorist in the White House. Wilson didn't often come here. No one knew him and no one cared. He ordered a pitcher of Bud Light and grabbed a couple mugs before sitting down with Jeff.

"What happened, man?" Wilson asked

"I saw you over by some lady screaming her head off. I grabbed Fred by the arm and told him we needed to leave immediately. He wanted to go over to where the lady was but I pushed him all the way to my car arguing. We got in and I started telling him where I've been. I had my window down and a sedan came up alongside. It must have followed us. I pulled my head back just as someone fired a round. Fred got hit in the side of the head. The car took off and I pulled to the curb. I got out and walked away as it came back and one of the guys got into my car with Fred. He did something or got something out, and then jumped back in.

They came back this way but didn't see me. I walked back a few feet to stare, hoping others would see me as a spectator. When enough people got there, I eased out of the crowd and saw you pull into a driveway. I left them and walked back to your car to wait."

"How did the story start about his wife cheating on him?"

"I heard he had a letter in his pocket. Do you think it was meant for me?" Jeff asked, "Do you think he was going to kill me and plant it on me?"

"Did you forget to invite me to your wedding?"

"I'm not married."

"There's your answer. They probably expected to grab you again and kill him, which suggests at least two teams. I'll be right back."

Wilson exited the bar through the kitchen carrying a glass of beer. He came around the corner outside and found a guy squatting beneath the men's bathroom window, looking at the parking lot. He quietly reversed directions, going around the other side and found his other half. This one was leaning up against the building looking around the corner towards the Jeep. Wilson quietly stepped up and snapped the guy's neck, allowing him to slide down the building. Afterwards, he poured his beer on him and walked away. To anyone getting close, it would appear it was someone who drank too much and passed out.

When Wilson came back in the kitchen, a burly fry cook confronted him.

"What the hell are you doing?"

Wilson replied, "You should be more concerned about the perv under the men's bathroom window."

After a few minutes, Wilson observed the burly fry cook and three-other large bikers talking. The cook pointed to Wilson as they walked outside. Wilson paid his tab and told Tompkins it was time to leave. They walked out to the Jeep. On the side of the building they had a clear view of a confrontation that was about to start outside the men's room. They climbed into the Jeep as the bikers were putting their boots to the man's face and head. Another biker appeared to be deliberately breaking the man's fingers. It looked painful.

Jeff said, "Man, what do you think that guy did?"

"Probably some perv looking in the window of the men's bathroom," Wilson replied.

They drove down the road and he decided he needed to get some cash, some new phones, and a new vehicle. He removed a trac phone from his bag and made a phone call. He asked for $75k in large bills and five new trac phones. He was told to wait one hour and head out the Pulaski highway to the Dunkin Donuts in Perryville. His instructions said to use the drive-through, place an order for coffee, and ask if they can change a $100 bill. Everything would be in a white bag. The person on the other end reminded him to call the boss.

Wilson made one more call.

"I need to place someone," is all he said. "I'll call back in five minutes."

Wilson had to stash Jeff. He had to be protected at all costs. When this was over, it was going to be Wilson's word against someone with a lot of horsepower. Producing Jeff would be his trump card to a bizarre story.

He called back in five minutes and had a location. Wilson drove for ten minutes and pulled up in front of the Rhodes 101 Stop, a gas station. He pulled around back and took Jeff up the backstairs. Under a planter was the door key and they went inside. Wilson turned on a few lights and told Jeff this was his home until further notice. The refrigerator was stocked, he had cable-TV, and there would be protection 24/7. No phones. Stay put. Do not go outside. Wilson said Chavis would be back that night to check on him and his security. He walked down the stairs and eyed the two men sent for protection before getting back into the Jeep.

Back on the Pulaski highway, he found Dunkin Donuts. At the window, he handed a woman a $100 bill and was handed a hot coffee and a large white bag. She was dressed in a business suit and had a nametag stating "District Manager", but it had no name. He got his change and drove off.

It was time to buy a new car. He missed his truck; the Jeep was okay but the Jeep had been followed so it needed to be left somewhere.

He continued into town and left the Jeep in long-term parking at the Landmark Parking lot. He cleared out the GPS Nav system and emptied the white sack into his quick bag before walking away.

Streetlights were on and everyone was rushing to get home after work. He walked down the street and over to Sport Chevrolet. He knew exactly what he wanted. He purchased a new black Tahoe by paying cash and drove South.

It was 10 PM when Wilson arrived in Great Falls.

The Old Brouge Irish Pub had been around since 1981 and was a favorite local gathering place. Annie Chavis was a Lumbee Indian from Pembroke, North Carolina and had grown up there making her penchant for dark beer and Irish Bars an anomaly to me. She was seated in the far corner with her back to the wall and her bag at her feet when he walked in. There was a frosty pitcher of beer in front of her. He was not sure what looked better to him: the frosty beer or Annie.

Chavis flagged down a server and asked for another cold glass as Wilson sat down. "Any food tonight?" the waitress asked.

"Fish and chips," Wilson replied.

"Shepherd's Pie," Chavis chimed in.

"Yuk," he said.

Annie began laughing. Her laughter made him realize just how much he had indeed missed her.

"Hey, Wilson, I'm compromising on the beer with your Bud Light, alright? You know I prefer Beamish Stout."

Their waitress returned with a cold glass, poured his beer and left. They raised glasses and nodded before drinking. It was fun to be together again. Actually, it was really great. He should never have let Annie go.

"You go first. Tell me how things went," he said.

"Tracy was a darlin' as usual. Married now by the way. We're in. She called in and set a hook for both your name and Maria's. I bought her breakfast and she went back to work. I walked around the monuments. I wanted them to know I was back. God knows there are enough cameras there."

As they talked, he wondered if Annie missed him as much as he had missed her. She called Tracy and had her check the logs before they left.

After Annie hung up, she said, "You are hot my friend. I don't mean just to me. It was all Agency and there is some inner-argument about you. There was also mention of more ends."

"Ends" was another name for deaths. If a project or assignment resulted in two deaths, it was referred to as two "ends."

"Jeff ran into a situation today on the Mall by Lincoln and I had to take out a shooter. I'll be on someone's camera. It was quiet enough so I was able to get away before the police came. Unfortunately, they followed him and his Section Chief and killed the Chief about twelve minutes later in the neighborhood where the mansion is. I do not know if they had folks there or

133

they followed Jeff into the area. It might be burned. We will have to recon it later if we are going to go back. I was not far behind them and grabbed up Jeff, before they could.

"I called in and got him placed afterwards. He has eyes on him 24/7. I would like you to check it out when we leave here and make sure he is tucked in for the night. He's above the Rhodes 101 Stop in Perryville."

"They still are using that one?" Chavis asked.

"Apparently so."

After they ordered another pitcher of beer, he had to ask the question.

"Why was it so important you wanted people to know you were back?"

"I dropped out of sight a few years back because my private contractor turned on me. I did them a favor by taking out Griselda Blanco in Columbia, when she was down there, something they could not do. Everyone was afraid of reprisals to their family so no one would touch it. Hell, at one point she was the 'Godmother of Miami' for the drug trade you know. I welcomed the challenge. I guess they decided they no longer needed me after that. Instead of shaking hands and saying piss off, they sent two teams to take me out. Assholes. I was on holiday in Gibraltar. I went wild when that happened. I left them worse than I needed to. I wanted them to have a huge mess and PR problem before I fell off the grid. I spent a year after that doing everything I could to bring Congressional oversight to their company."

"You still have a temper, don't you? Who says you don't play nice?" He laughed. "So what you're saying is we both are hot now. I have the Agency after me and you have who?"

"They've changed their names so many times, it's been hard to keep up. Reynolds, the billionaire, still owns them. I think the latest name is Graystone. Believe me, I have thought about taking him out but there would be no one left to appreciate it. Besides, his security is stellar. It would take two of us." She looked over at him, smirked, and laughed.

"Who do you work for Wilson? Tracy said you have not been NSA for some time, but no one will cut off your access. You seem to float through the system. A lot of systems is actually what she said."

"I'm sworn to secrecy." They both laughed and he leaned over and told her. He paid the tab; they grabbed their bags, and walked out to his new ride.

In the dark, he took out a two phones and $10k for Chavis.

"You okay going back to the mansion?" he asked her.

"I am if you are. Let's sweep it and come in from the water together. We will drop over the wall and do a 360-degree before going inside. I need to ride with you. I returned my van to the rental lot I appropriated it from."

They tossed their bags in the Tahoe and headed back across the river. It was like old times.

Wilson drove the Tahoe down the street and parked about 500 feet back from Jill's mansion. They hopped out with their bags and moved over to the side of a house where they could maintain visual on the street. Nothing was moving. It was 1 AM. They sat hunched like this for a half hour and then split up. They met at the water's edge of the mansion. Everything was quiet. They had decided earlier not to take out the cameras because they would want them operational later when they went inside. If company was there, it just made it more interesting.

S. P. Mowre

They finished combing the grounds and entered through a side-garage door an hour later. The only car inside was a Bentley. They gave each other the nod, flipped a coin, and Wilson won the toss. He entered first, followed by Chavis. The house was as secure and empty as they had left it.

Chavis went outside, walked back and brought the Tahoe in. Wilson went to the security room. He wiped the hard drives, then re-set the recording and activated the outside perimeter.

They looked at each other. A lot of time had passed, but each one still saw the feeling in their eyes. Annie looked down and laughed. She said she would take the first watch so Wilson grabbed a bed. After four hours, they changed and Chavis slept.

After breakfast, Annie used a trac phone to call Tracy. Tracy wanted to meet, the sooner the better. They agreed on Arlington again, same headstone in one hour. Both of them armed up, grabbed their bags, and started out in the Tahoe.

Wilson pulled a pass from his bag and showed it to the guard, enabling them to drive into the cemetery. They parked about 100 yards from Audi Murphy's headstone and walked back. Both of them knelt and said a short prayer while the other watched. There was no bigger hero buried at Arlington than Murphy. As he wished, his headstone was very small and unremarkable. Most Americans visiting the huge monuments had no idea what he had meant to America in the dark days of WWII. They were more concerned about their iPhones.

Tracy walked by wearing a ball cap and moved to the back of the amphitheater. They joined her, Wilson on one side and Chavis on the other.

"Well boys and girls, you're still alive so it's a good day so far. I feel like a double agent meeting with you two. You were the

136

subject of some chatter this morning. Not that that's big news to the two of you. Chavis, you have some visitors from South America. Two to be exact. They came through Miami last night and had sponsorship. You know who their handlers were? Agency boys from Psy-Ops. Here is the problem. These two are killers from the Medellín Cartel out of Columbia. Our Director cannot believe the CIA Directorate would blatantly violate U.S. laws, not to mention pissing off this President. He is asking for collective Intel before taking it to the Bureau and the White House.

"With that kind of risk, something huge was happening and the NSA had missed it. We were directed to back up and take a better look, inputting 'Chavis'. He had not seen Chavis' handprint on the Blanco take-out, but knew Greystone was contracted for it. He recalled this huge dust-up in Gibraltar where Greystone almost lost their congressional funding and explored that calling in some favors. Turns out Greystone tried to take out the agent who had taken out Blanco. Huge mistake. He figured it was probably Chavis since she had disappeared off the grid right after. How is the guessing so far? Do not say anything yet. Lo and behold, we find both of you in different cars within a half-mile of 'reported violence' where the Agency exerted authority over locals to handle. My boss said where one goes, so goes the other, which is why we didn't stop looking when we found one of you.

"Then, we came across information that the Bureau is missing two agents from its D.C. office. We do not know if it is related or not, but it is being looked into.

"One last thing. I don't know how this ties in, but the Maria that you are looking for Wilson, Maria Styletti? I learned she was admitted under the name of Laura Charles to Woodville State."

They sat there for a moment taking things in and assessing threats.

Tracy spoke again. "Look, I have to make a formal report of our meeting and what transpired after I leave here this morning. It is nothing personal. I say that because I do not want you to tell me anything you do not want to see in print. I love you both."

"How old is the Intel on Maria?" Wilson asked.

"Not sure. It came in pieces over this last week," Tracy replied. "There's been nothing since."

She stood up and started to walk away. She stopped and said, "Be careful. Directors are becoming involved and you know our government. Problems are ended only when folks disappear." She pulled her cap down and left.

Chavis waited until Tracy left before saying, "Look Mike. We're not going to get Maria out if we have your friends and whoever breathing down our backs. Let's get those assholes first."

"If two came, it would mean that they have at least that many more, Mike. The Agency will use their resources to point them in our direction so let's help them out. Let's go rent a house and have a house-warming."

They jumped in the Tahoe and stopped in Falls Church at Hertz Rental. Chavis rented a van with full insurance, this time in her name, and swung around to pick him up. He tossed both of their bags in and climbed inside. She handed him a local paper and he looked for a house. After about fifteen minutes, he found a townhome that had woods behind it on Raymond Court and used a trac phone to call the listing agent.

She happened to be in the area and was available to meet then so they drove over to the other side of town. Wilson remained in the van.

The house was decent enough and furnished. She was asking $2,608 a month with a $300 damage deposit and the previous month's rent. Chavis told her she had just cashed a check and asked if she could pay cash.

Ciara Green, the agent, was efficient and all business. Chavis signed the papers using her real name, paid Miss Green the money, and walked out with the keys. They had a home now; well, Annie did.

The next stop was Bank of America on Arlington Boulevard. Annie opened a safe deposit box under her name with her new address. She was officially a resident.

The bait was set and in less than twenty-four hours, everyone would know where she lived. This also meant they had half that time to formulate a takedown plan.

They grabbed a pizza at lunch time from Flippin Pizza and headed to the mansion to plan. The streets were clear going in and they moved warily down into the mansion drive. Wilson did a quick check and returned signaling Chavis to put the van inside next to the Bentley.

Inside he checked the security room and everything looked good. The hard drives were cleaned. He also activated the exterior alarms once more before sitting down to eat.

The more they thought about it, they both knew it had to end here. Too many people were getting involved and once politics set in, it became very difficult for bosses to save face. Chavis had run out of favors and had no immunity.

Wilson, on the other hand, worked for someone who chose to remain anonymous. The fact that he had never taken political positions was the reason why he kept his job so long. Even now, he had no dog in 9/11. He did not because he refused to entertain even thinking about it. He earned his reputation by staying out of these things. It was crazy. He just wanted to save Maria and get these whack-jobs to back off. Any killings had been defensive; well, most of them. These would be too. Their plan had better be good.

"Michael, this does not matter to our mission, but I am just curious. How much does this Maria matter to you?"

Wilson stopped chewing in the middle of a third slice and smiled.

"She's a friend, a neighbor with benefits if you will. Besides, you know my requirement. She can't cook steak."

Annie laughed.

Wilson suddenly thought of something. He told her of his plan, saying, "Why don't you take the van and scout Woodville. I will take the Tahoe and go pick up Jeff. We'll meet back here."

They picked up the Tahoe and each headed out in their own direction. Chavis had a four hour drive each way. This gave Wilson plenty of time to pick up Jeff and return to the estate to finish planning with him.

He took the I-495 Capital Beltway and soon merged onto I-95 N. After an hour on I-95, he exited onto MD-222 and came out onto Broad Street. Within minutes he was on Pulaski highway and soon pulled in behind the gas station. Wilson looked around and walked into the Bay. He knew the manager. There had been no unusual activity and no breaches.

Wilson went around back and nodded to the two agents seemingly working on cars. He went up and knocked on the door.

Jeff let him in and pleaded his case to leave. He was bored. He was a federal agent and shouldn't be in hiding, he argued. Wilson smiled and agreed it was time. They went down the staircase and jumped into the Tahoe. When the Tahoe swung onto I-95 S, Wilson told Jeff his plan. After an hour of discussing ideas, they exited onto VA-7 for the mansion. Wilson pulled over to the curb and handed Jeff a silenced .22 from his bag.

"Stay in the car, stay low and keep your eyes moving. I'm going to get a little exercise and make sure we're still safe. I'll be back in twenty minutes."

Wilson crossed the street and began his walk. He didn't see anything extraordinary. He walked around the mansion's grounds, spoke to the neighbor, and returned.

"Let's go," he said jumping back in the Tahoe. He entered the mansion grounds and had Jeff open the garage door. Inside was the van that Chavis had rented. A note was on the wheel.

"Get down," Wilson yelled to Tompkins. They both hit the ground and came up holding weapons. Wilson eased around one side of the van while Tompkins did the other. The garage was clear.

Wilson read the note through the driver door window. It said:

"Sorry for any concern. Took the Bentley and bought a dress. I know – me in a dress! Going to inquire into admitting a loved one into the hospital – A"

"Stand down," Wilson said shaking his head. They closed the door and went inside. They checked the security room, and he saw Annie alone, backing out of the garage in the Bentley. He cleared the images from the hard drive, then re-set it and activated the exterior alarm.

The guys met in the kitchen and scouted the refrigerator for a cold beer. Jeff was happy to finally be doing something.

Annie was just merging onto I-376 W/US finalizing her pitch about why she preferred Woodville. Driving the Bentley was to add to the veracity of the story she was going to tell. She had used a trac phone and called ahead. She identified himself as Mrs. Rubio MacPherson and demanded to meet with the Chief of Staff, Dr. Chu Lee. Woodville did not exactly have a great history. Since 1852 mental patients and others were kept there for "treatment". Eventually it was turned over to the County and finally, the State. Its history and access were dubious at best. For Chavis' plan, that made it even more perfect.

She pulled up in front of the administrative offices and got out of the Bentley. Dr. Lee was standing on the steps.

Watching his face, she could see the Bentley had the desired effect. She was greeted like a VIP. Her neckline was not lost on the doctor either. It made her want to squeeze his head, but she shook hands with him instead and went inside. After all, it was why she bought the dress she told herself.

"Dr. Lee I have a very delicate situation that I believe you might be able to help me with. My husband has suffered from depression and has recently become paranoid. He thinks everyone is out to harm him. His delusions sometimes exceed more than the average person can even comprehend. I'd like to have him brought down and examined with the possibility of a long-term commitment."

"Certainly, Mrs. MacPherson. My facility is equipped to do that. We would need to have all his prior records and a referral letter from his last psychiatrist before the entry examination, you understand. Then we have a battery of tests to see if a long-term commitment is an appropriate treatment."

"Doctor, I am hoping to avoid the public embarrassment. I would prefer to have him admitted under a name of my choosing so my daughter would not be able to remove him in the middle of the night, so to speak. She loves her daddy dearly and all she wants is to have him home. We need to get him thinking straight first. I have been known to donate excessively when I am pleased with results."

"Really, Mrs. MacPherson, we have more than adequate facilities here for commitment. At night, there is one male orderly at the reception desk and one on each floor as well as a night nurse. We do not like to bend the rules because it is difficult to maintain state accreditation. I'm afraid the conditions I outlined really need to be met even given a hospital donation later or not."

"Allow me to be more candid, doctor. I do not want others treating my husband. I just want you. I know your time is valuable and perhaps you will need to go off the clock at times to do this. Would $10,000 a week compensate you?"

Dr. Lee looked down, put his fingertips together and gleefully smiled.

"Certainly, Mrs. MacPherson, I didn't mean to imply I was refusing the admission nor that I couldn't accommodate your wishes. I was merely outlining policy. We are willing to work individually with patients and their families to achieve the best result. When can you bring your husband in for, ah, treatment?"

"That's what I like to hear. How about tomorrow night? I need to get Mr. MacPherson in as soon as possible. Here is an envelope with some petty cash for any expenses needed for such short notice. I think there is $5,000 in there. I will have my staff call you and make the arrangements, tomorrow morning. Course, I will have my security detail deliver him, if that is all right with you. This way the hospital need not pay to have extra security on hand. No sense in paying for others when you have your own, I always say. We'll be in touch."

Lee followed Mrs. MacPherson outside and shook hands reassuring her he would exceed all the family expectations for privacy.

"Oh, by the way. You didn't tell me. Where will his room be?" Chavis asked.

Dr. Lee pointed to the top floor.

"He'll be on the third floor. Now he won't have the entire floor as we have one more VIP at the far end. But they will not see each other. In fact, each one has their own elevator and fire staircase. I oversaw the remodeling myself last year. They are actually suites. And don't be concerned that one is better than the other. They are exactly the same. Both suites will be served their meals at the same time too. You can select from our room-service menu. Your security can eat too, if you choose to have any of them stay. There are actually two guest rooms and the master for family accommodations. Five-star, if I do say so."

"I guess you answered my last questions, Dr. Lee," Chavis said.

Lee opened the driver door for her and she climbed inside. She started the car and put the window down.

"There is one more thing. Our arrangement will remain strictly confidential, am I right doctor? You will tell no one. I don't want the other VIP to even know. It would prove a violation of our trust and I would have to have my attorneys serve you if that were to happen."

Dr. Lee's smiled disappeared. He could see thousands of dollars disappearing. While the 'others' were insistent about knowing every patient being admitted and being given advanced notice of anyone being assigned to the other suite, they made it clear they would not be staying long. The amount they paid

SECRETS ARE DEADLY

had been a flat sum of $50,000. Screw them. He could make that up in five weeks with MacPherson's money.

"There is no need for attorneys here Mrs. MacPherson. Frankly, they will probably leave by the end of this week. Yes, our arrangement will remain between us."

Chavis drove slowly out like the pompous bitch she hoped she had portrayed. She drove off in the opposite direction she had arrived. The map she looked at earlier had shown a heliport. Chavis wanted a good look before she returned to Falls Church.

Over four hours later Chavis pulled into the mansion garage and found Wilson waiting.

"I've been curious all day since I found your note. What was the Bentley plan and how'd it work?"

"Here I thought you were anxious to see me in a dress for the first time."

It was his turn to laugh. He pulled her arms and turned her around slowly. She was gorgeous and she knew it. She gently pushed him back with a soft expression he had never seen before, then she gave her hair a toss and laughed, and the moment was gone.

"Greed is always a good thing because most men never disappoint. The doctor was one of them."

She shared her plan with him and the fact that Oakdale heliport was 3.7 miles from the facility. That was great news. He would arrange for a chopper extraction for Maria.

Annie went inside to change while he made the call. It took longer than he thought. He had to provide a callback number good for seven minutes.

Inside, Jeff did not hide his gaze as he eye-balled Annie walking by in her dress. She was stunning.

145

"Don't say anything Mr. Tompkins if you ever want to talk again with a full set of teeth. I'm going to change and I'll expect a cold beer when I come back." She kept moving.

Wilson came in, erased the hard drive of Chavis returning the Bentley, and re-set the exterior alarm. His phone rang and he answered. Wilson and Chavis agreed on everything except Maria. Maria had to go where no one could get to her, Wilson insisted. The call ended and he returned to the living room. Annie had changed into jeans and a tee shirt and was drinking a beer. Her .45 was at the small of her back. This was the Annie he knew.

They discussed their roles. Chavis and Wilson had always been a team. They never had a doubt where the other was or how long it would take them to handle something. Jeff Tompkins was an unknown and tonight that was where their focus was. They needed to know his limitations.

Jeff sensed where the conversation was going when Chavis told him they needed to know his background.

"I might not have your job and I'm not allowed the leeway you are to kill people. That said, I would not hesitate to put down any of these guys. I joined the Marines as an officer out of college. I served two tours in Iraq before joining the Bureau. You have to think on your feet in either job and sometimes rather quickly to remain upright. I will say it again. You don't need to worry about me carrying my load."

Wilson spoke first. "I'll forgive the part about you being an officer in the Corps," He laughed. "Our concern ,Jeff, is that we need to double-tap these guys and keep going. Everyone. We will not have time for the whole put your hands up, drop your weapons, and surrender deal. That will get you killed."

Chavis added, "With regards to Maria, entry teams have a job to do. We are not an entry team Jeff. We are a termination team. We are going to go in and kill everyone around her and bring her home. I want you to understand that. This will not be a police action. I do not care how you justify it later, in your own words. Just know going in that is what we will do. If we do not do that, those same guys will come after us. If we do not do that, someone has to do something with the 'prisoners' we take. Make no mistake about this. I have no immunity. I cannot have witnesses. I'm not going to prison because you wanted to come along. If I have to, I'll kill you too."

There was an uncomfortable silence in the room. If there was any illusion of dating Annie Chavis when this was over, Jeff no longer entertained it. Wilson looked at Chavis while Tompkins got up and returned with three beers. Wilson started laughing out loud. Chavis was serious. He realized again what he had been missing in his life.

"I got it. You can count on me. I have been abducted and tortured and have seen my boss killed. If it was not for Wilson, I know I would be dead. Just tell me what needs to be done."

Wilson discussed the house they had rented. Come morning the Agency tags would notice the names and the address. The fact that a safety-deposit box was rented would provide further proof of a long-term residence. The Agency did not have time on their side and would strike as soon as it got dark. They were desperate.

He suspected the two Columbians and a few contract boys would be the ones going into the house. There might or might not be Agency boys ringing the area a block out. They would not torch or blow it. They needed to know Chavis and whoever was with her was dead before they flew back home. This would be hands-on; it was personal.

Jeff added his thoughts about how he envisioned it playing out. It all depended on timing and coming in from outside the circle. They needed to peel back each layer until they had trapped the teams inside the house. There was no doubt how that would end.

Chavis spoke about the hospital. Getting in was already taken care of. Extracting Maria and getting out was the unknown. They would improvise. She produced a copy of the remodel plans the hospital had filed with the county. Chavis had found them on line and printed them up.

Money had been saved by not removing the center elevator shaft from the second to the third floor. The opening had been covered by sheet rock and was directly centered to both rooms. This meant that they could come in there. It was also another avenue of escape if needed.

Wilson said there would be a chopper waiting for Maria. They just needed to get her to the heliport afterwards. They would regroup immediately at the mansion after. No exceptions. Chavis brought in both quick bags and took a few items from both under Wilson's watch, to furnish a backpack for Jeff. He handed Jeff her MP 5/10, which was a newer version of the MP-5 but fired 10mm rounds. She also weighed him down with four thirty round clips. She put in a couple flash bangs and a trac phone and they were good to go.

They spent the rest of the night telling stories and listening to Tomkins tell war exploits. They did not share any of theirs. He had more experience than they thought and it was evident now they would be going in almost like-minded.

Chavis suggested they pack it in and get a good night's sleep. Tomorrow, they would go over things one more time, eat well, and wait for darkness to fall. She motioned for Wilson to wait.

"Mike, things have been kind of breaking rather quickly. I feel like nothing but time has passed. You?"

"Yeah, I am good on this Annie. I like the plans and having you back beside me. It's all good. These guys have no idea of the shit-storm coming their way."

"When we get her back, Mike, do you want me to leave?"

"Look Annie, she's just a friend, a neighbor that needed my help. Once she's safe, she still will be my neighbor and still will be my friend. We do not have what you and I have. I will never have that with anyone in my life, Annie Chavis."

"I'll take the first watch," she said and exaggerated her walk for his benefit as she moved over to the large sofa.

Wilson turned and left the room for bed. He wanted to say more, but he was not certain how to say it. He just knew he did not want Annie to go away again.

Annie turned around watching him walk away. One of them was going to have to make a move one day. They were thirty-two years old, for Chrissakes. Men. Maybe she should charcoal that steak when this was over.

9. RESCUE LEADS TO SLAUGHTER

At Woodville, Maria was not so lucky. She had lost two fingertips, both nails on her big toes, and had swallowed more water than she knew possible. She had not slept in days. IVs containing truth serums and God-knows-what were connected up to her night and day. She did not care anymore. She just wanted to die. She could not think about anything else. Death would be welcomed. She could smell her hair burning; she pulled and twitched as they stuck her with needles and laughed. As daylight started to enter the room, she passed out again when they affixed electrodes and sent current to her frontal lobes. Just before she did, she hoped this was it – she hoped she would die.

She remained unconscious all day. Her captors received a call after darkness set in from a "Mr. Smith." Smith stated that the "warrior" had rented a house in Falls Church and would be taken out in a few hours.

"What's going on there? If she is not awake – wake her up. I am pissed. You guys are letting this drag on and on. Every time I call, she is being moved or is sleeping. What is wrong with your team? Do I have to replace them? It is imperative I know whom she gave any information to or if she sent copies to anyone. We have not had to pay the Judge a visit, but one Bureau person has been taken out and one is missing. There is also the fact of her U.S. Marshall-cop-neighbor out there somewhere. We'll find that son-of-a-bitch. He's had the crap scared out of him so we think he'll trip up soon. I have another team ready so you better get the results. When you're satisfied, make her disappear."

There had been a lot of promises made that good things would happen when his boss, William Baldwin, became Deputy Director. They had lost a few people the past few days over some top secret 9/11 file O'Neil had never seen.

O'Neil had handled the wet work and lately there had been a lot. He heard a mewing sound and turned around to the bed where their prisoner lay. O'Neil told the nurse to get busy and move her into a chair. They were none too gentle about it either, strapping her shoulders, waist, and legs to it. Styletti's eyelids were pulled opened and taped to her forehead. She could not even scream anymore. This time nurse Jackson gave her a hug and said it broke her heart to do this and Maria should just tell them what they wanted to know. So far Maria had told them she had left a phone message to Mike Wilson who she thought worked for the Marshall's office asking for help and copied files to her computer. She claimed she didn't know anything else. She hadn't told anyone anything. The nurse looked into her eyes. They were lifeless. That might be until she removed one. She reached up with her scalpel and told Maria what was coming and how it would feel. O'Neil had never seen someone getting their eyeball taken out while they were still alive and pulled up a chair to watch. Tears ran down Styletti's face but still she made no noise. Her tongue was swollen from biting it but that wasn't why. She continued to stare at the flowing black Ninjas entering the room believing death was coming. She welcomed it.

The nurse placed the scalpel next to her face and a hole opened up … on the nurse's forehead. She closed her mouth and slowly her legs bent until she hit the ground. Then two holes opened up on O'Neil's shoulders; he too, fell slowly to the floor with a surprised look. The two other guards went down with holes like rupees on their foreheads. Every person in the room had holes. She was dying; she was losing reality. She passed out with her eyes open.

Wilson had purposely wounded O'Neil so they could "visit". In less than two seconds of listening and observing, Wilson determined O'Neil was the one to keep alive – for now. He took O'Neil to the side and bent his hand backwards creating as much pain for him as he could without forcing him into unconsciousness. The first hand snapped, breaking. O'Neil gave up William Baldwin's name in record time. Wilson patted him on the head and then snapped his neck. Death was too good for this guy, but he didn't have time for anything better.

He walked over to Maria and cradled her for a moment before removing the tape from her eyes. It pained him to do so. Tompkins made sure everyone of his captors was dead and in flex-cuffs with duct-tape over their mouths and eyes. The duct-tape was just in case one of them was not dead. There would be no shout-outs.

Downstairs Chavis assuming her role as the bitch, Mrs. MacPherson, began moving from floor to floor taking out the staff. There was no emotion about it. It had to be done and it was her job. She returned to the front desk and waited in case someone came through the doors unexpectedly.

Chavis watched Wilson appear with presumably "Maria" over his shoulders with Jeff at his back. The four of them moved outside. Jeff was told to take the Bentley back and they would meet him at the mansion.

Chavis drove the Tahoe with Wilson and Styletti to the heliport. A black chopper was on the tarmac and two bodies on the ground. When Chavis eyed that, she put the Tahoe into a spin and they took off. Wilson grabbed her shoulder from the back seat and told her it was okay. Go back.

"Didn't you see? Your people are on the ground. Someone took them out," Chavis shouted.

"Those aren't our guys. Here are our guys."

A Marine Corps AH-1W Super Cobra attack helicopter was landing. The pilot kept the engine powered up. The side door was thrown open and it waited hovering just above the deck. A sniper team stepped out from nearby buildings and gave Wilson the okay sign.

Seeing this, Chavis turned around and pulled in. Maria was loaded onto the chopper and pulled onto a gurney by Navy Corpsmen, who strapped her in. The sniper team climbed aboard. One member leaned down and above the noise shouted to Wilson, "The General said congratulations on a job well done". He handed Wilson a small folded piece of paper and saluted. The chopper flew out. Wilson put the paper into his pocket and watched them lift off before getting into the Tahoe.

The house on Raymond Court had been secured. Jeff's phone call had set things in action. Wilson had made one himself. The Bureau's Hostage Rescue Team were all inside. Deputy Director Sean Joyce was on site. On the first floor, inside, were two very dead Columbians with ties to drug trade. Two more were in the kitchen. Automatic weapons and handguns were at their sides. One HRT team member was wounded and in critical condition.

Outside on the ground in flex cuffs were several men that had been disarmed. They were claiming federal law enforcement. They all had the same phone number to call. There were eleven of them; one was wounded. That was why Assistant FBI Director Joyce was on the scene. Well, that and the fact that the President of the United States told him he would be.

Local FBI picked up Dr. Chu Lee who had remained at home. He had invoked his right to remain silent and was driven to a cell at the Chesapeake Naval Brig. It was noted he was there at the request of the Director of the FBI and was to have no contact with anyone. The Commander himself was ordered to sign the acknowledgment. Three hours after that, eleven subjects, one with bandages, were placed there as well. The entire bloc was off-limits to anyone below the rank of naval Lieutenant. For the first time in brig history, two naval Lieutenants stood guard.

Under Presidential special order 223-9, the Marines airlifted Maria Styletti to the USNS Comfort T-AH-20, a Navy hospital ship during the night. She was to be treated by the Navy and guarded around the clock by Marines. The Admiral, himself had to sign the acknowledgment. The Navy was to do everything they could for her, including therapy.

Jeff drove home to the Mansion relieved that it was all over. He would contact the Chief's wife in the afternoon and help arrange for his funeral. Outside, he exited the Bentley and heard a sexy voice say, "Nice ride sailor." It was Agent Carlson. She looked nice. He smiled, closed the door, and she shot him in the head.

* * *

While Chavis was driving, Wilson thought over the events once again. Things were coming together; some not quite as he expected. His thoughts went to Maria. How badly had they damaged her and why? Would the President keep his word?

They pulled into the Mansion driveway and entered via the garage, closing it. The Bentley was there. They went inside each carrying their bags, Chavis to the kitchen for a beer, Wilson to the Security room to wipe the hard drive and re-set the exterior alarms. As he moved towards the computer, he heard the shower come on down the hall. Chavis or Tompkins were washing off the night, no doubt.

Suddenly, gunfire broke out from the area of the running shower. Wilson thumbed off the safety of his .45 and came face to face with the lovely Jill Carlson. She shot him in the chest and the .45 in his hand blew the smile off her face. Wilson tucked and rolled, which saved him from the next blast. Behind him was one of the Columbian hit men. He fired a shotgun that partially scalped the prone Wilson. His ear was barely hanging on as Wilson put two rounds from the .45 into the shooter's chest that opened a view window on his backside.

He waited and no one else appeared. There were no other sounds. As far as he knew there might be three other people in the house: the other hit man, Jeff, and his Annie. Thoughts flooded his mind as he bled from his scalp and the hole in the right side of his chest. All dead? Who traded the gunfire? Jill and one of them? Or was it one of his team and the hit man? Was Jeff in on this? Had they already killed him? They had to have been inside when they got home. Damn it. He had been careless.

Annie shouted out, "I'm coming and I'm going to kill everyone of you, do you hear me?"

It made him laugh. It was the last thing Wilson did before he sighed and closed his eyes.

Annie had taken a swallow from a cold beer and started the shower in the bathroom just before the shooting started. She was getting ready to get in when she decided she felt better just having her shower gun, a Glock .40, on the towel rack. It was a habit. She wrapped herself in a towel and went back to her room to get it out of the bag. She returned to see a Columbian walking into the bathroom carrying a shotgun. Fricking perv! She shot him in the back of the head, twice before the body hit the ground. She ducked back around the corner when she heard two shots; one was from a .45. She thought it had been the second shot. A shotgun blast followed that. Two more rounds followed it from a .45. Okay, that was good. That had to be Mike.

Annie Chavis waited. There were no more sounds. No one spoke, so she did.

"I'm going to kill everyone that's within the sound of my voice. So help me God."

She deliberately moved slowly so she could listen as she grabbed another pistol, one in each hand and left her room.

10. CAMP DAVID

Wilson woke up almost five days later fighting heavy sedation. It was a struggle to look around the room before he fell asleep again. He had been placed in a medically induced comma.

"Welcome back Frankenstein," a familiar voice said.

He turned his head, opened his eyes and found Kenny Johnston, a Navy Corpsman that had accompanied him overseas more than once. They were close friends. Last he had heard, Kenny, had been on a hospital ship in the Middle East.

"Annie Chavis? Is she okay? Is she?" Wilson asked, "And, Agent Jeff Tompkins, any word?"

"I'm not supposed to know, but I overheard. The Bureau found Agent Tompkins in the trunk of the Bentley at the place they found you. He had been shot in the head by a weapon issued to Agent Carlson, according to the gun match-up. They also found Carlson dead, who they said you shot. There were no signs of Chavis, but they were told that a woman fitting her description remained in the area until the ambulance took you away. And again, an hour later at the hospital, a 'Mrs. Wilson' checked on her husband. They confirmed it was her by the hospital security videos.

"You probably should not contact Chavis anytime soon though, boss. The Bureau is looking for her. Seems that both the Director and Assistant Director in the CIA's Psy-Ops were assassinated from a shot estimated at almost a mile away, the day after you were badly wounded. Not many people can make that kind of shot, let alone snap two consecutively. They were exiting one car when it happened at a black tie event. Their driver was killed too. The rounds were from possibly a special military sniper rifle, you know, like you guys tote in your quick bags. At least that's the word." He smiled.

Wilson closed his eyes alternately worrying about Annie and Maria. It was two more days before he opened them. The cool water that was used to bath him was responsible. The corpsman put a syringe to his IV. He blacked out again.

When he woke up this time, he remained awake. Someone had bathed him again, shaved his face, and dressed him in pajamas with the Presidential seal. All the tubes and reminders of his being hurt were gone from the room. FOX news was on. It was covering the funeral yesterday of a friend of the President's being buried at Arlington with full military honors. The Presidential motorcade was present, but the media was keeping its distance out of respect. Across the bottom of the screen a ticker ran. It said Gus Hokold had passed away over the weekend from cancer at the age of 85 at the National Naval medical Center in Bethesda. He was a retired Marine Corps General that had served at the behest of several Presidents. General Hokold had no living relatives.

Kenny entered the room with two Secret Service Agents dressed in casual clothing. "The President is here, Mike." They stood aside as President Mark Lombardi entered the room.

"How are you feeling Mike?" he asked.

"I'm doing just fine, sir. Thank-you for sending the chopper. I ran out of options."

"You never run out of options, son. It is why you work for me. In a week, Corpsman Johnston here will get you moved to a place of your choice. Take a few months off. Get back on your feet. Then come see me. I used some favors cleaning up matters I had no role in, but you did, if you get my drift. We need to talk about those. I should tell you that both you and your friend Miss Chavis are clear of any involvement in any chargeable activity over the last few weeks. Also, I've been told that banking has been taken care of and deposited into that bag of yours. Anything before I leave?"

"Can we talk privately for a moment, sir?"

The President looked over at the agents and nodded. Kenny and both of them left the room.

"Maria. What was so important that her research lit such a firestorm?"

"I guess we'll never know. She died of a heart attack three hours after her airlift. I was told they did all they could. I wasn't going to say anything until you got better."

Wilson looked at the President to gauge what he had just been told. He nodded and closed his eyes. The President left the room. He lay there angry with himself. He should have gotten to her sooner.

Kenny returned and noticed the change. "What can I do for you Mike?"

"I want out of here. I have a place to go. Get my pants." He sat up and swung his feet over the bed, and dizziness set in.

Kenny put his hands on his shoulders and pushed him back lightly. He covered him with a sheet.

"I guess it won't be today. Bring me my pants though, will you, Kenny?"

The pants brought to him were new.

"What happened to my clothes I was wearing?"

"I was told that everything you were wearing had blood on them so they were discarded. You have new clothes but I oversaw the sizes – they should fit, boss."

"Paper. I had a piece of folded paper in one of my pockets, a note. Any idea where it might be?"

"I have no idea," Kenny said and looked around the room. The Secret Service has your quick bag, but it's locked up somewhere. At Camp David, even you don't get to walk around armed.

After a week, Wilson was on his feet. He used Camp David to jog and work out with Kenny at his side for the next two weeks. He had no idea where Chavis had gone, but he had no doubt she would come back if he called. He would go to her too, if she reached out. It was just unspoken. Meanwhile, Wilson had one thought on his mind and that was to get home. Well, to Gus' home. He could use his computer skills and remaining time off to find out about the property. He needed to do something with it. There was no way he could buy it. He wanted to, but he did not have that kind of money. Then there was Prince. His thoughts went to Gus-town next. They would need income to survive.

He told Kenny he would be leaving in the morning. They discussed how to contact each other over dinner and retired for the evening. Wilson headed outside and took his last walk through the forest. Camp David was really a military installation in Maryland's Catoctin Mountains, known as Naval Support Facility Thurmont. As a "Presidential" Navy base it was guarded by a specialized Marine detachment.

As Wilson walked, he noted cameras and heavily armed Marines deployed throughout. He thought about government. Take this place for example. It was built in 1935 following the depression as part of the public works act – built by the WPA for federal employees and their families as he understood it. In 1942, President Roosevelt visited and decided he would name it Shangri-La. He decreed it for Presidential use only. He took it away like a dictator for his own use. Later, another President, Eisenhower, decided he wanted to name it after his grandson, David. It was renamed Camp David. No one voted on any of these actions.

He had completed several assignments for the current President, Mark Lombardi. He was loyal to him and it was returned many times over. As the President had said, he never really ran out of options. Not many people could say that. The "blank check" came with an understanding though. In addition to the non-disclosure secrecy agreement, Wilson could not show any interest in or take any part in politics. That suited him anyway. He did not know everything Presidents did or wanted to do. Maybe even JFK's curiosity or actions crossed the line somewhere. He would never know because the American public was not allowed to know. There was a conversation somewhere, in a room, in a building maybe like this, and JFK was terminated with prejudice. The government had its secrets.

9/11? That one bothered Wilson. But then again, it bothered many Americans if one was able to talk alone with them. He knew where the answers were. He also knew he would not live to see that the American public knew, if he pursued it. He had to let that go. The President trusted him and the President had a long reach.

Who made the 9/11 decision? There were so many red flags, but like with JFK, no one really cared for long. No one spoke up. Maybe there was a shadow government. The fact that NORAD, our Air Defense, was given a plan to rehearse a high jacked civilian plane attack on the same day as a real attack, just didn't resonate. It kept the Air Force in confusion; most fighter pilots and radar technicians thought the air traffic was simply part of the war game until it was too late. It was overwhelming and defeating.

He walked full circle and came back to his cabin. He seldom had doubts but something nagged at him. It was not 9/11. It was like a scab that needed scratching. He would work it out; he always did. What did he miss? Wilson went inside and sat down to watch the Tonight Show. However, he sat there oblivious to the monologue.

Finally, he yawned, turned off the TV and climbed into bed.

In the morning, a Marine guard and a Secret Service Agent appeared at his door. The Agent was going to transport him; the Marine had his quick bag. He looked into the mirror and his head had been shaved leaving a Frankenstein set of stitches on one side. His ear had staples in it. Nice.

Wilson asked to go into town and be dropped off at his D.C. condo. He climbed into the SUV with the agent and was handed his quick bag from the Marine with strict instructions to not open it until he cleared the gates. Finally, out on the road, he removed his .45 and chambered a round before putting it at the small of his back. The agent looked over at him with indifference. He probably figured if his head looked like this, he would be racking a .45 about now, too. They arrived an hour later. He had the agent drop him off two blocks away. He looked over and saw his new Tahoe. Thanks Annie. He would walk in. Things might be over, but Wilson remained cautious. He scanned the neighborhood and other doorways and windows for any threat. He was about a half a block from his front door when he decided to enter via the balcony at the rear instead. Course it required some work and a little physical strain for a guy that had been shot, but he was up to it. He walked back and came around through a couple yards standing below his place. He thumbed the safety off the .45 and tossed his bag up. It landed with a good thud. Next, Wilson climbed onto the bottom condo deck rail and walked hand-over-hand up the drain spout he had reinforced last year, onto his balcony.

With the .45 in one hand, he jimmied the sliding glass door latch using his other and a thin metal strip from his wallet. The door opened and he reached for his bag pulling it inside.

Well, well. Someone still had hard feelings. Wired to the front door was a package. Upon closer examination it had a pressure switch and a bubble level as a back-up trigger to about six ounces of C-4. At least someone only wanted to kill him and not all the neighbors. Wilson went into his quick bag for a set of wires, a tiny set of locking pliers, and an even smaller screwdriver. He sat down and whistled while he dismantled his homecoming gift.

When there's a gift, one of the elfs usually likes to stick around and see if he got you the right present. Sometimes Santa required it. How did he miss this guy? Now that this was done, he decided to go back out via the balcony with the quick bag and hunt the elf. It took him another twenty minutes before he spotted 'her'. She was dressed like an average Betty, but her demeanor and mirror-watching gave her away.

Ever mindful of the last time he approached a female in a car, Wilson casually walked down the street and as he passed her, he asked for the time. When she lifted the wrist she wore her watch on, he grabbed onto it, leaned in, and pointed the .45 into her lap. Anyone looking out the window would think he was looking at the time on her watch. He told her to smile and she did. She thought she knew what was coming. She did not. He ordered out of the car. They walked up to his front door and he handed her the key. Wilson told her to open it. There, he saw it. Fear in her eyes. Just a flicker, but it was there. She turned to him and told him what she knew. It was not much. Her name was Robin Shane. She was forty-three years old and had two kids. She was not a field agent, but was given this "opportunity" to watch and report back confirmation of his death.

Wilson told her he had dismantled the bomb and ordered her again to unlock the door. She complied but she moved like she didn't believe it. Tears ran down her face. They stopped when the door opened. Wilson pushed her inside and shut his door. He set his bag down.

"Who gave you the order? Who are you supposed to report back to?"

"Curly Doman. Curly gave me the order but I saw Rudy Spencer, our department head, talking to him. They argued before Curly came over to me and said to grab my coat. I'm pretty sure it was Mr. Spencer's idea. Curly left me in the lobby for fifteen minutes before returning with a box. When we got here, Curly got your front door opened and pulled the bomb out of the box he brought. You know the rest."

"What agency do you work for?"

"CIA – Psych ops."

He checked her purse and pulled out a cell phone. Sometimes the agency analyzed stress in voices. He was banking they would be over-confident today.

"Call Curly and tell him you signed for a package that UPS just dropped off for Wilson. Tell him you tore some of the wrap off and you can see your logo stamp on a file folder. Ask him if he wants you to read it or take it home for the night?"

She made the call and said "yes" a couple times before she hung up.

"He's coming over here. He told me to stay put and don't let go of the file."

"Here's what you're going to do, Robin. You are going to go back to your car and sit behind the wheel. When Curly gets here, you are going to wave hi to him. I am going to have a scope on you, got it? After that, I'm done with you."

She started to walk out his door, but turned and said that Rudy Spencer, Doman's boss, was coming too. He handed her their bomb less one wire and she closed the door behind her. She carried it across the street as if it was a newborn baby.

Next, he pulled out his sniper rifle, assembled it and lay down on the entryway to his front door. No one was at Maria's so it was very unlikely anyone would come up this far and see him. He sighted in on Robin Shane's car. She was sitting once again behind the wheel looking unhappy. They waited.

Almost forty minutes passed before a gray Ford sedan pulled in behind her car. She waved to them in the rear-view mirror.

He waited for the passenger to get out and shot him in the head. Pop – the driver went next. As Robin reached for her gearshift to put her car into gear, he shot her right above the ear.

Three down and no one seemed upset in his neighborhood. He took out a camera with a telephoto lens from an end table and snapped off six good shots of the carnage. This time, he left the bodies and called no one. Let them deal with this. He needed to get going. When he disassembled his rifle and repacked his bag, he found the folded piece of paper the Marine on the helo had given him.

He opened it up. Inside a small safe deposit box key was taped with an address. Interesting. The note read: "Congratulations on a job well done". He would have to deal with that later. He dropped the key into his bag and headed back to the Tahoe. It was time to head back to Gus' house. On the way, he needed to trade his ride in for another Jeep.

* * *

Presidential special order 223-10 came one week later. The order was to have her sedated and flown from where she was to the NAS Gaeta, a U.S. Navy Base in Italy. She would be met by a security detail and taken to a villa. The Navy's responsibility ended when she arrived at the villa. There would be no log entries. It could not come soon enough for the Admiral.

* * *

She woke up in a sunny bedroom with a view of the Mediterranean Sea. Things were so pretty. The walls in her room were bright yellow as was the side of the house that came into view. There were two bright bouquets of flowers. She remembered being on a Navy ship or maybe that was a dream?

"Hello Maria. I am happy to see you awake. My name is Cathy Robinson, I'm your nurse, your companion, and your security detail for as long as you need me."

* * *

Outside on a hilltop looking through binoculars lay Chavis. She was not able to see into the rooms of the estate due to reflective window coating. Moving Maria onto a Navy hospital ship had been a secure move. Certainly telling the Admiral where and when she would be going three weeks later by communication was not. Tracy at NSA had never been told to stand down. She discreetly continued to note information she intercepted that she thought was related to them. Since she had her own job to do each day and was alone, there was no way she could get details. When she heard the President directed a female be moved off a hospital ship to a base in Italy, she tagged it. The term "sailor" was not used so it had to be a civilian.

Tracy also told Annie that Mike had left Maryland and went back to his condo. Some sort of dust-up happened there and Mike vanished. Chavis was surprised things were continuing but Mike would be okay. This last news led Chavis to the Mediterranean villa. She thought she might as well settle in and observe what the government had in store for Maria. Italy was a beautiful place, even if you had to be there by yourself. She assumed Mike had full knowledge but if he did not, Chavis would. She would find a house to lease and maybe take some time off. Once settled in, she would return to observing. Maybe some of the locals might know something about that yellow house too.

* * *

Mike completed the transaction for a new 2021 Jeep Rubicon Unlimited with a soft top at Alexandria motors. The dealer was surprised he was trading in a new Tahoe but Mike explained he needed something more nimble. Even optioned out, the Jeep's price difference was considerably less. Carrying his quick bag, he found a green one with nearly a $20,000 dollars price difference. It had everything he needed.

He drove out and headed to the bank to cash his check. Cashing a check for $20,000 was not an in and out event. The teller confirmed his identification and called the dealership to confirm the check. The manager introduced himself as John Rodgers and attempted to talk him out of carrying 200 $100 bills out of the bank. The manager soon acquiesced. The federal forms were filled out since it exceeded the $10,000 banking limit. Mike was given an old canvas bag and he exited the doors leaving the manager shaking his head.

When he approached his Jeep, two guys came off his fenders where they had been resting. They were not professionals. These two looked like street punks, gang-bangers with baggy-ass pants. It was trouble he did not need, but he was sure they were going to give him some.

"Nice Jeep. You must have money," the bigger of the two said.

"Yeah man, you must have some green on you. Maybe in that bag?"

Wilson had his .45 at the small of his back. He did not want to use it so he thought he would try to joke his way out of it.

"Well, guys, I did have money but then I bought my new Jeep. Now, I don't have anything," he said.

He stepped in to unlock the door when the small one made a grab for the canvas bag as the big one went to body-slam him into the side of the Jeep. It just was not their day. Wilson saw it coming. He reached out with his ignition key and jammed it as far as he could into the left eye of the biggest one, twisting it, while kicking out. His foot connected with the right knee of the smaller one at the same time and he heard a snap. Both went down screaming and swearing. He stepped back and with great force, he stomped his heel on the right hand of the big one on the ground. He kicked back hard and broke the big guy's shoulder at the rotator cuff. Now, he would be blind in one eye, be hunched over, and have an unusable hand for the rest of his life. He leaned down to the smaller of the two as if to shake his right hand. Instead, he snapped it back breaking it just above all his fingers. This was a great tactic that affected one's ability to hold a weapon of any kind, forever. They would make a good pair walking down the street bobbing and weaving trying to be tough six months from now. He straightened up.

The manager came out, "Are you okay? I called the police and they have a car nearby. They should be here anytime."

Wilson heard sirens about the same time as the manager finished speaking.

"Oh, I'm okay. These guys here could probably use some medical aid."

He climbed into his Jeep and started it up. As he backed out, two police cars arrived blocking his exit. The officers jumped out and drew their guns. The manager walked over to them, pointed to the guys on the ground and then back at him. One of the officers was a Sergeant and he started laughing. They holstered their weapons and the Sergeant walked over to Wilson as Wilson climbed out of his new Jeep.

"What happened here?" the Sergeant asked.

"Well, I'm not sure. These two guys were leaning on my new car when I came outside from banking. We had a disagreement over my giving them some money and they ended up on the ground. I don't want to press charges, Sarge."

"Can I see some identification?"

"Yeah, I'm Michael Wilson," he said, extending his hand. They shook hands and Wilson gave him his I.D.

"You know Mr. Wilson, I don't know who is luckier, them or you but I guess it's them by the story John told me. You must be an expert in martial arts or by looking at you, maybe you are a Marine?"

"I've had some training." Wilson smiled and looked down.

He heard more sirens and a third police car arrived followed by a fire truck. The paramedics jumped out and one brought over a box to the two on the ground. Wilson could see some splints in one of his hands. The other carried a backboard.

The third officer asked the Sergeant what he wanted him to do.

The Sergeant turned to Wilson and asked, "Can I call you by your first name, Mike?"

Wilson nodded.

"Mike, you don't have to press charges. The County of Fairfax will do that for you. We would like to see these two men go to prison for a while. No one will testify against them because they are afraid. Guys like these two have friends if you know what I mean. Now, I don't think Mike, that idea bothers you, am I right? The part where they have friends."

"You're right about that. I'm kind of in a hurry or I would have expressed my displeasure more to those two."

He smiled. "Officer, take Mr. Wilson's statement and let him go. And Mike, I'm assuming that you have papers that allow you to carry that big gun under your shirt, right?"

The Sergeant handed the officer his I.D. and didn't wait for an answer. Just before he got into his car, he turned and looked at Wilson.

Wilson asked the officer what his Sergeant's name was. He might need a favor or a friend in Alexandria one day.

It took the officer almost 20-minutes to take his statement and release him. Since he was delayed, Wilson thought he may as well input the address for the safe deposit box key and see how far he was from it. What was another twenty to thirty minutes?

Wilson packed the bank canvas bag into his quick bag and pulled out the paper and key. He entered the address and found it was just outside Waynesboro, Pennsylvania. It clicked and knowing Gus was a General and a friend of President Lombardi's, he realized he would be headed to the Rock. The Rock was almost two hours away. It would put him in there around 1 PM. It was a place he had only heard about.

He left the bank and headed out to I-495 via the Capital Beltway going back almost the way he came that morning from Camp David. He wasn't certain if his name was cleared to get into the Rock, but he was going to try. In a few minutes, Wilson took the I-279 Spur merging onto I-279 N. The Rock was Raven Rock Mountain Facility and more secret and probably secure than even Camp David. They were actually six miles apart. The Rock was also known as the "Underground Pentagon" since it was the National Military Command Center. Its largest tenant was the Defense Threat Reduction Agency with full military operations centers for the Army, Navy, and Air Force. He turned onto I-70 at exit 32 towards Hagerstown and now, was probably thirty minutes out. If he was going to turn back, now would be the moment. Up to now, Wilson presumed the "General" the Marine was referring to was Gus. Whatever Gus wanted him to have should not be a concern to anyone. If it was another General, it might be a problem. As a rule, he never entered a secure facility unless he knew what he was going in for and even more importantly, if he was going to get back out. The CIA had no jurisdiction here. The military loathed them so he thought his risk level should be minimal.

He circled on MD-66 to MD-64 which became PA 997 and stopped less than a mile down the road. He removed his .45 and placed it inside his bag. He placed the Jeep's purchase order in the glove box and put it in gear driving towards the main gates. He passed several imminent threatening signs about trespassing and live ammunition. "STOP DO NOT PROCEED OR YOU WILL BE SHOT" read the last one. He stopped there.

Two uniformed military police officers approached him through a side gate as two Marines in combat gear held MP-5A2s at the ready. Two towers had thick bulletproof glass that were heavily tinted. Each one had a barrel sticking out through a gun port in his direction. He raised his hands and waited.

"Sir, you are trespassing on a U.S. Military Installation. If you do not have credible identification and a credible reason for being here, you will be placed under arrest. Do you understand me?" the Corporal asked.

"Yes, I do."

The Corporal continued, "If you do anything other than I tell you, you will be shot. Do you understand me?"

"Yes, I do."

"Do not move. Keep your hands in the air. We are going to search you and your vehicle."

"I have weapons and cash along with another I.D. in my bag," I said.

"Thank you, sir," said the Corporal who told the other MP to take control of Wilson's quick bag before searching the Jeep.

The Corporal searched him, removed his identification and asked for his name.

"Michael Wilson."

"Who do you work for Mr. Wilson?"

"My apologies Corporal, but that is classified."

The other MP cleared the Jeep and carried his bag just inside the gate they had emerged from. He returned and backed the Jeep up the road about a half-mile before returning and handing the Corporal the key. Wilson guessed that was in case the Jeep was wired with explosives or other electronics. The Corporal placed handcuffs on him. Large concrete barriers hissed and dropped down in front of the gates as they opened. The Marines trained their weaponry on him as a Humvee came out. The Corporal placed him inside between two other MPs and the driver returned the Humvee to inside the compound.

He was a little disappointed to see a metal construction trailer was going to be their destination. While he had seen pictures of the Rock, he had never been inside the mountain and he was hoping to get a chance to do so this time. The Humvee stopped at the side of the trailer where the two MPs removed him and searched him again.

They took him to the front of the door and a Marine Colonel stepped out. They stepped back letting Wilson go and saluted. He returned the salute and ordered them to remove the handcuffs. When they did so, he directed them back to the Humvee to wait for his signal.

"I am Colonel Richard Kreiling. To what do I owe the honor, Mr. Wilson? Why are you here?"

"Colonel, I was given a key that I believe came from Marine General Gus Hokold, along with this address and instructions to seize the contents of the box it went to."

"You do know the General Hokold died, correct?" he asked.

"Yes sir. I watched on TV as the President attended his funeral."

"Well, I knew Gus and he would not have told you to drive on over here and walk right in. We both know that. Start over and this time just tell me why you are really here."

"Colonel, I was befriended by General Hokold several weeks ago. I have been taking care of his German Shepard, Prince. Gus, I mean the General, left, I guess for the hospital and I never saw him again. I was on a mission, a classified action, when a Marine on a Super Cobra gunship handed me a piece of paper and said it was from the General. His exact words to me were, the General said, "Congratulations on a job well done." I looked at the address and knowing the General, I surmised the box the key went to was located here at the Rock. That's all I got."

The Colonel signaled the MPs in the Humvee.

"Cuff him, blindfold him and take him below to level seven. I'll meet you there." He walked away as one put handcuffs back on Wilson and the other pulled out a blindfold. The MP tied it so tight the headache was immediate.

He was led across the compound and through a series of gates. He heard them clear five sentry points before they entered an elevator. Counting and listening was what Wilson did when he was someone's prisoner. He had quickly become the Colonel's prisoner right now.

The doors opened after six seconds and the temperature was considerably cooler. Two people stepped in and took him out and the doors closed. The voices were different. He was directed verbally to move ten steps forward and wait. He complied and heard them walking away. Soon, a door to his left opened and he was brought inside. Machinery was humming far away and there were no voices. His blindfold was removed and he found himself across a table from the Colonel. Two Marine Captains flanked him. When the handcuffs were removed, the Colonel invited him to sit down. Wilson rubbed his eyes and his temples as he sat.

"Mr. Wilson, I had the statement you gave me up top transcribed. Read it and if you agree, please sign it. On page two is a listing of all your property including your Jeep. If you concur everything is accounted for, please initial next to each item and sign the bottom."

Having enlisted in the Corps, Wilson knew it would be faster if he did what he was told to do. He wasn't that confident that the President could find him at this point if the military didn't want him found anyway. He took his time, signed and initialed everything before sliding the paperwork across the table to the Colonel. He signed it and pushed it to the Captain on his left who signed as a witness. The Colonel then pushed it to the Captain on his right who signed and notarized it. "Legal," Wilson thought, but why?

The two Captains left the room leaving just Wilson and the Colonel. Wilson noticed cameras in two corners and suspected the room was mic'd. Someone was watching and recording. He was good at sitting and did just that. They looked at each other for several minutes before the door opened and a First Lieutenant poked his head inside.

"He's been cleared Colonel. Cleared by the Commander-in-Chief." The Lieutenant pulled the door shut.

"Mr. Wilson, seems you know important people. Until I am relieved of my duties though, you will continue to follow my orders, is that clear?"

"Yes sir," he replied. Now, Wilson could feel his confidence return. If the President or his staff had been contacted, they would start here if he never saw daylight again.

"Colonel, do you know where General Hokold's box is or a box that his key went to?"

He must have had a buzzer under the table. The door opened, two MP's came in and put a blindfold back on him. They stood him up and the three of them left the room and got back on the elevator. This time he was not handcuffed but he had no illusions about being confined. He counted three seconds again as they dropped down and stopped. The doors opened and he was led

Twenty-three steps into another room. From there, he felt he was taken into a tunnel or well-insulated chamber.

He could feel the area's dimensions were larger than he thought by sounds bouncing. Time echo counting of the same sound or sounds was a reliable way of finding out how far something was from him. It took a knowledge of equations, good ears, and practice, but he had gotten out of some tight situations in the past doing just that. His blindfold was taken off and he was stunned at what he saw.

He was inside the biggest vault he had ever seen. One wall was all safety boxes with a ladder on rollers to access the ones near the ceiling. Colonel Kreiling entered and handed him a key tied to a large brass D-ring.

"This is my key. You'll need it to unlock the box using your key as well. As part of our internal security procedure no one knows what box number is in use and by whom. At least no one here does. You are welcome to start. If you get tired and you need to rest, there will be a Sergeant outside this door and he will take you to a bunk. If you stay over or work into the night, we will of course feed you in the morning. In any event, when you unlock the door to the General's box, ask the Sergeant to notify me. We will need to blindfold you to release you above ground. You must wait until the door closes behind me to begin. Any questions?"

"No sir. Let's hope I get lucky." He turned and left. It reminded him of the safety deposit area in a bank. No one remained in the area with him.

There were hundreds of boxes; thirteen hundred according to his math. He was pretty sure he was being jerked around. Someone had a list. His connection to the White House probably was what warranted only minimal assistance. Commander-in-Chief or not, often those in the military felt the President created more problems for them.

He started with the bottom row and after an hour decided to try to make it interesting using a grid. It was twenty minutes into this grid, nearly an hour and a half later, that box 789 came into view high above. What the hell, it was his number, he might as well give it a shot. He moved the ladder over, climbed up, and inserted the Colonel's key and the key the Marine had given him. It opened.

Wilson climbed down slowly as the box was eighteen by twenty-four inches and more than twelve inches deep. When he reached the bottom, he placed it on the nearest counter and walked over to the door. He was able to turn the knob and when he opened the door, the Sergeant stepped into view. Wilson told him he removed the box. The Sergeant invited him to take a step out, directed him to wait, and picked up a wall phone presumably to call the Colonel. He spoke quietly before hanging up.

"Do you or the Colonel need to witness any papers leaving?" Wilson asked.

"Yes sir. This is a top secret national security facility and all papers must be viewed by two command officers before leaving in someone's possession."

Wilson turned around to go back into the room. The door had closed and was locked.

"Sir, without exception, no papers will leave the room you are in. General Order 203-7."

The Sergeant unlocked the door and let him back inside the vault room. Wilson opened the box and began reading. After, a quick perusal he did not want anyone to see or read these papers either. He was certain Gus would feel the same. That fact made it even more perplexing that he would use this facility for turning them over to Wilson. Gus of all people would know the rules. Wilson started over with a personal letter inside a white envelope.

Mike,

I knew I was dying when I found you under my tree. What I did not know immediately was that I would choose you to carry on my legacy. Prince and I decided hours later. I trust you will. I found out your identity from my computer that you no doubt already have found. Your files say you are a true patriot; that you are a brave and honorable man. Some men take their Nation's secrets to their grave. I will take most of those I know to mine because I don't want you to have to carry the burden of knowing as I did or knowing what I did. You will have your own soon enough.

Good men struggle between right and wrong or better said, the appearance of right or wrong. Something may appear wrong if one does not have all the facts. Keep an open mind. Before I went into Bethesda, I brought all my papers here, where no one would ever read them, in case you wanted to walk away. This is a facility like no others in terms of secrets. Only thirteen boxes have owners. Not every one of the locked boxes you have gazed upon has contents, but all thirteen owners have a box number they personally chose. They must take an oath to pass their key on to someone in the military that meets specific criteria. If the owner dies before that selection is made, his box is located and the contents removed and destroyed. No reading or judgments are allowed. The remaining twelve select a replacement. I am passing my key onto you. You are number thirteen. I will talk about that in a moment.

All my real estate holdings, monetary funds, and Prince are bequeathed to you if you accept. You will be contacted by an attorney with civilian paperwork within 10-days of your visiting here. Prince is a very special unique animal. We experimented for years breeding what we hoped would be excellent guard dogs for our facilities worldwide. There were many problems, many tragic animal deaths and funding of the "Prince" program was shut down. One of the chief scientists knew my support of the program had been without question. He also knew how much I loved animals. He gave me the last two vials of serum he had been working on and hoped I would preserve it as all paperwork was destroyed per regulations. I froze them at the house. One remains. As you know, I used the other.

I located a wolf's den one day while walking outside my town. You can imagine my surprise but then I thought of the Prince program. I set out some meat that I had baited but the wolves were too smart. They circled it but probably sensed something was wrong. One night I lie out in the field and shot the female with a dart containing a mild tranquilizer. Unfortunately, the male had circled behind me and attacked about the same time. I had to kill him. I felt badly and hoped I could inject the female perhaps creating another life for the one I had taken. It was 63-days later exactly that she gave birth to Prince. In the early evenings, I would watch through binoculars as his mother frolicked with him. They had a great relationship. She was very nurturing. His colors were beautiful as he grew blacker every day. She didn't return one evening and the next day Prince was bawling like a baby when doc found him wandering I guess. He gave him to me since I lived alone. I recognized him right away. You know the rest.

I have never been afraid of death, but I didn't want to leave Prince. Please take good care of him and Prince will take good care of you.

The number thirteen. Well, Mike, I am one of the thirteen-Patriots. There is one for each of America's original colonies. We are what some people call the "Shadow Government" that books and people have speculated about for years. The Rock is our location. It is where we meet, where all our documents are kept. No one, not even Presidents, know we exist with certainty, including the men and women that work at this facility. It is an awesome responsibility. There will come times when you will ponder if you are doing the right thing for America. Our decisions are not easy ones to make.

The Declaration of Independence was just one of the founding documents. It declares our right to change, alter or even abolish our current government if it is a threat to our Nation or its people. As continuing, founding fathers, we remain vigilant in our duties and the protection of our freedoms.

We have stepped in on three occasions, none of them occurred at our hands. July,1947 when the "greys" crash-landed one of their ships in Roswell, New Mexico; November,1963 when JFK met his death; and

September,2001. There are no related documents to those moments as we judge none before us. Those involved in September, 2001 are still being dealt with. I will tell you that the CIA created Bin Laden. Rynard Speer was one we later learned helped mastermind the attack.

My trust in you is well placed. Good luck son."

Other papers indicated code words needed to enter the main gates and each floor. Gus suggested Wilson change his access code at home. If he accepted this responsibility as Gus hoped he would, he was to utter the phrase "The best of days are here to come" to Colonel Kreiling when he exited the room. If he didn't, there would be no visible change. Lastly, he was to shred any papers he no longer needed and to secure the remaining ones inside this box.

You left me no real choice now did you, Gus? Wilson thought. Sure, Wilson could turn him down. However, he would never leave here alive. Gus knew it and knew Wilson would too.

Enough was said from Gus that he really didn't want any part of this. He was never involved in politics. He avoided knowing any pieces or names that played a role in any cataclysmic event. Wilson had been in tight places before. He thought about this one, its exits, and his probabilities to stay alive. He also realized that Rynard Speer was the man Wilson killed over in Europe which preceded and may even had precipitated all these events.

It seemed like a year had passed since that night he landed at Andrews and Jeff had picked him up. A lot had happened. Maria was dead, Jeff was dead, and for some in the CIA, their battle with him was still not over. He went from owning a small security company to an entire town of good people and a hybrid military wolf – all of them depending on him.

This wasn't for him. It wasn't what he wanted. He thought about Gus. This kind of responsibility – whatever it was – belonged with someone who had seen a lot. It belonged with someone who had walked among powerful people. It belonged with patriots.

He looked around and found a shredder. He shredded everything that had his name on it and put the remaining papers back into box 789. He secured it into the wall and moved the ladder to where it originally was.

When Wilson opened the door, the Colonel and two Marine MPs were in the hallway. The sergeant was gone. He handed back the D-ring to the Colonel without saying a word.

"Marines, place the handcuffs and hood cover on this man."

They placed the handcuffs on him.

It was then Wilson uttered, "The best of days are here to come."

The Colonel directed the Marines to remove the handcuffs and leave them alone. Once they were gone, he asked Wilson to follow him. They entered the elevator and rode up to the ground floor. No one paid any attention to them. Once at the top, Wilson followed him through a maze of locked doors and out into the fresh air of the compound. The sun was setting.

"Your Jeep is parked over there and your bag with all its contents is inside it. Over there is a guest complex. That is yours, sir, to come and go as you please. I will assign the Marine Sergeant that was below with you as your liaison. Please contact him before you arrive here for anything you need while you are here, and of course, when you leave. Sir, excuse me."

He saluted and walked away as the Marine Sergeant appeared.

"Sir, my name is Sergeant Trace Whiting. I am your go to guy, sir." He saluted.

Wilson saluted back.

"Can I call you Trace?" Wilson asked.

"Yes sir."

"Alright Trace. My first request is that you do not call me sir anymore. Call me Mike or Wilson or Wils. Can you do that?"

"I can when we are speaking privately if that's your request. Can I show you to your room Mike?"

"Can I leave? Can I just get in my Jeep and leave, now?"

"Yes sir. I mean, yes Mike. You can do whatever you please. I don't know if the Colonel was clear and we don't purport to understand how, but you have the equivalent rank of a General now, sir. I mean, Mike. Currently, there is no one that outranks you at this facility, sir.

"I'm outta here Trace. You seem like a nice guy, but I hope we don't see each other anytime soon."

"Yes sir, Mike." He saluted.

Wilson returned the salute and walked over to the Jeep where he noticed a small black and blue insignia on the windshield. Inside was his quick bag as promised. He started it up and put it in gear thinking any moment he would be shot in the back of the head. Instead, the main gates opened. As he passed through the guards came to attention and saluted him. He returned the salute.

He could not get down the road fast enough. First thing first though. He removed the .45 from his bag, chambered a round, and with the safety on, put it at the small of his back. He felt better and headed towards PA-997. Along the way he activated the nav system getting onto I-495 and headed for home. There was a lot to take in and he needed some sleep.

Wilson arrived home about 9 PM and twisted the pump. He drove onto the platform and rode it down. When the platform hit the bottom and the roof was in place, he quickly headed down the tunnel with his quick bag in one hand and the .45 in the other hand with the safety off.

Inside, the first thing he did was check the door. His hair was still in place. He left no room or hiding spot unchecked. In fact, he checked everything three times including the Jeep tunnel. Tomorrow, he was bringing Prince home. His home. Their home.

He slept fitfully. He would wake up and think about Jeff, and how he could have prevented his death. An hour later, he would wake up and think about Maria. He was certain she had died of fright. He was equally certain it could have been prevented had he not spent all the time here at Gus's. Maybe this is what he meant about "knowing" and things haunting you to the grave. Wilson didn't like it.

When daylight came, a cold nose awakened him. Prince had decided to come home on his own. Wilson sat up and gave him a little tussle until he pulled back. Okay. That was fair. He got up showered, dressed, and made breakfast. He poured just enough bacon grease over the dog chow to make Prince happy and set down a bowl of fresh water to go with it. Both bowls were empty in no time. When Wilson turned back around, Prince had vanished. The "ghost."

He went downstairs and powered up and logged into the computer. It flashed its five-minute warning. The first thing Wilson did was change his password. It wasn't real happy with that, but he managed to get it done and check his drop box. There was a request from Tracy to meet. It was the only nessage and more than a week old. He figured it was routine as there was no urgency attached to it. Since a week had gone by, he elected to get back to her in a few days.

He removed his smart phone from his bag and inserted its SIM chip. He called in and there was a message to meet the President that night at 10 PM in the Old Executive Building. Wilson confirmed he would be there. As an afterthought, he printed up the photos from the last assassination attempt at his condo. When they were dry, he folded them and put them inside his pocket. He was unsure of the direction his Presidential meeting might take and he might need the ammo.

The OEB was known to many as the Eisenhower Office building. It was a grand building completed in 1888. It was not a well-kept secret that a tunnel connected it to the White House. Wilson had used it himself a few times. During Pearl Harbor, the Japanese Diplomats walked its halls with FDR. Winston Churchill had graced its corridors. Some Presidents like Nixon even kept a secret office there. It was almost torn down in 1957, but better heads prevailed to preserve history.

With Prince back, Wilson felt more at ease and definitely believed the house was safer. He repacked his quick bag and put the .45 at the small of his back. He wanted to check in on Gus town.

It took him almost no time to get there and he only had to use the nav system once. The first thing he did was to stop off at Doc's. He gave Mae a hug and let her know he was back and Prince had come home.

"Mike, do you know what's next for all of us? I mean the town? Some people in town here had seen the President attending a funeral for a General named Gus Hokold. I guess they were friends. Our Gus's last name was Hokold. Is he gone, Michael?"

"I'm sorry Mae. I was in the hospital myself and saw it on TV as well. Gus had many secrets. Yes, General Hokold was our Gus. Your Gus. I need to find Doc."

"Well, he's over at the store visiting. He will be excited to see you, I know. Are you alright now? I mean you said you were in the hospital?"

"Yes, thank you. I was hurt but I'm doing just fine now."

He jumped in the Jeep and headed that way. Penny was out on the steps when he arrived. He suspected Mae had called her. She gave him a big hug and said doc was inside. Wilson walked in and grabbed a cold water. Everyone smiled and nodded or said hello. He asked Doc if he had a moment and stepped back out the door.

"What do you need son?"

"Doc, what happened to Jill, the FBI Agent?"

"Oh. She decided she would rather stay another day at the hospital then call a taxi home. I told her she could stay there or with Mae and I, but no way was I letting her take a taxi home.

We compromised. I drove her into Toms Brook where she had a fellow agent waiting for her. They drove off. Was that okay?"

"Yeah it was fine. You did just fine. Turns out she was a bad person and I'm still concerned about her compromising the town and the hospital."

"Are you sure, Mike? She seemed really nice."

"Oh, I'm positive Doc. She is no longer with us so I'm not worried about her. I am concerned about others. If you get any visitors, I want you to use the phone I gave you. Remember, put the chip in and call me; take the chip out. I will monitor that number. You can also send an email to me using my name at AOL. It's not a direct address, but it gets rerouted to me. Only use either one if you absolutely need to. Please."

Wilson went back inside with him and visited with everyone so they did not think he was rude. After all, he was contemplating being the "new Gus". Who was he kidding, he was the new Gus. He just did not want to say it aloud yet.

At 8:30PM, Wilson stopped near the Treasury Building and spotlights lit up his Jeep. Secret Service searched him, removed his .45, and asked him to state his business. He told them he had a meeting with the President. One got on his radio and others used a dog and mirrors to search his vehicle inside and out. His quick bag was taken into custody and he was told he would get it back when he left. They directed him to park across the street at the Willard Intercontinental. Other Agents met him there and he put his Jeep in the underground parking. They accompanied him back down the street. At exactly 9 PM, he was standing at the gates to the OEB. Another plainclothes Agent came out to get him.

"Sir, the President is down the hall, this way."

He was let into the office that the Vice President uses. President Lombardi was seated in a large wing chair.

"Come on in Mike. How are you?" They shook hands as the President stood up.

"I'm fine sir. I feel great. How are you and the Nation doing sir?"

He chuckled and replied, "Well, the Nation is doing just fine despite my leadership. Look, Mike, that was some nasty business the last few weeks, wouldn't you agree?"

"Yes sir, I would. I did not choose it, sir, if that is where this is going. In fact, the FBI Agent that got killed contacted me first about my neighbor. Things just snowballed after that."

"This *is* where it's going. The Director of the CIA has been clamoring for your hide. He cannot understand why so many of his agents are dead, two Directors assassinated, and you are not in prison. He also said something about national secrets possibly being compromised. The Director of the FBI complaining about CIA people sponsoring hit men inside our borders is the only thing keeping him from going public. So you see, Mike, I have two agencies at each other's throats because of the activity that you involved me in."

"Sir, if I may. I completed my assignment and flew home. Agent Tompkins reached out to me. Before I went home, I checked in at the office and then went to my house. While I was sleeping my alarm went off and I found two intruders."

"You know, Mike, sometimes people get paranoid. Hell, even the President of the United States gets paranoid. I was wondering if maybe you should have seen what they wanted before starting the gun-play."

Wilson looked at him. No one especially the President of the United States was that stupid.

"Okay. Okay, Mike. That was a dumb thing to say. You have every right to shoot intruders in your home. However, shooting a woman in her car out on the street? Why couldn't you just have called it in? Maybe I could have ended it. The mess over in Falls Church cost a Bureau Agent his life and the arrest of many CIA Agents. There's some doctor screaming about his rights and wanting to sue us for keeping him in the naval prison while this is still being sorted out."

"I don't know what to tell you, sir. They are still after me."

"Come on, Mike. I have the word of both Directors that this ended before I placed you at Camp David."

Wilson produced the photos of the carnage outside his condominium and handed them to the President.

"These are after your Secret Service Agent dropped me off the very day I left Camp David," he said.

The President looked at each one carefully and the photo date on each backside. He sighed and walked over to a shredder. It did its work while he looked at his watch. He turned around and looked at Wilson.

"This ends now, Mike. Tomorrow morning, the Director of the CIA will hand me his resignation. There will be some Directorate staff leaving as well. In the morning, I want you to meet with the Bureau's Director. You will fill him in on what you can leaving me out and this evening's visit out. Are we clear?"

"Yes, Mr. President, I am clear."

"Do you know what National Secrets the CIA is referring to that they think you have compromised or might be about to compromise?

"I'm not sure we should have this discussion sir. It's about 9/11."

"I am the President, Mike. I'm clear to read any document or know any secret. It's a little insulting that you would think you should know and not I."

"With all respect to you personally and the office, sir … I'd like to keep you alive."

The President's facial expression changed. He looked down and took a few minutes to think what Wilson had just said, before responding.

"I'll accept that for now. Let's do our best to keep each other alive. I'm not angry about this, Mike. It just takes a bit of arm-twisting and tax-payer money to make this go away. I'd rather use those favors and resources for the Nation, if you get my drift."

With that, he stood up. The door opened as if on cue, and he shook Wilson's hand nodding to the Agent. He walked out and the agent closed the door behind him. Wilson guessed he wasn't leaving.

"Mr. Wilson, I am the President's senior agent on duty tonight, sir. My name is Agent Andy Reynolds."

"Hi Andy." They shook hands.

"Sir, the President has conveyed to me that you are to be a guest over at the Blair House tonight. You have an early meeting with the FBI Director and he wants me to insure that you keep that meeting." He smiled.

"Fine, let's go to the Blair House."

"Actually, Mr. Wilson, one of my Agents, Luis Garcia, will accompany you. Should you need anything, anything at all sir, please open your door. Luis will be right outside."

With that, he spoke into his wrist mic and Agent Garcia appeared from a side alcove.

The two of them walked out and over to Blair House. Wilson had never been inside so spending the night was fine with him. He did not like having a baby-sitter, but after all, the President had given the order.

There were several uniformed agents outside and two inside when they walked in. The two inside greeted him as "Mr. Wilson" having been told he would be arriving, he guessed.

Luis tucked him away in a very nice suite. He was not sure what he was going to do for a shave and clothing but he was certain the Secret Service did. He would see what the morning brought.

Wilson took off his clothes and climbed into bed. He was just starting to replay the President's conversation in his head when he dozed off.

The next morning, Wilson put his pants on and walked to his door. As promised when he opened it, Luis was sitting there. Next to his chair was a small pile of new clothing and a shoebox with tags on it, and hanging onto the doorframe was a suit. Wilson pointed to this and Luis nodded, handing him the stack of clothes and dress shoes. Wilson grabbed the suit.

"Bacon and eggs over medium alright sir?"

"Throw in some toast and coffee, Luis and I'll be a happy guest."

He found toiletries in his bathroom. He had just shaved and showered when there was a knock on his door. A butler brought in breakfast along with a paper.

He finished eating and read the Washington Post. Luis knocked and asked if he could come in just as Wilson finished tying his tie.

"Sir, the Service will provide a car and driver for you when you're ready."

"Luis, I think I'd like to walk over to the Hoover building this morning."

"Sir, the Service will provide a car and driver for you when you're ready – at Andy's direction. We are to make sure you keep the appointment sir."

"A lot of fuss is going into this meeting wouldn't you say, Luis?"

"It's not my place to comment, Mr. Wilson. The car will be outside in five minutes. Whenever you're ready." He closed the door.

Wilson gave himself a glance in the mirror. Kudos to the person that picked out his clothes. The sizes were correct. He looked like he just walked out of GQ magazine except for his short hair growing back and where plastic surgeons has sewn his ear back on. Probably only he noticed the ear. They really had done an excellent job.

A black Tahoe with blacked-out glass waited out front with a driver. An agent jumped out and opened his door, "Good morning Mr. Wilson." He nodded and climbed inside to find Andy reading the paper.

"Well, well. Does the Service ever sleep, Andy?"

"Good morning Mr. Wilson. I trust you found our arrangements for you satisfactory?"

They both laughed.

He looked over at the White House and wondered if the President was watching. As he said, a lot of effort had gone into this meeting.

The drive over took less than five minutes even with morning traffic. They pulled into a secure area and Andy got out when Wilson did.

"The Director is expecting us promptly, Mr. Wilson so we'll go in through this entrance here."

He motioned into an area where the public was obviously not allowed. Andy walked up and showed his credentials. At his request, Wilson produced his driver's license and the sentry signed them in. They were escorted inside by someone he assumed was an FBI Agent. He looked younger, than Wilson. Once inside, Andy waved him ahead of him through the security checkpoint. Wilson removed his belt before walking through, having nothing but his tags in his pockets from the new clothes. Andy, on the other hand, removed a SIG P228 and two fully loaded magazines from somewhere on his body and placed them into a nearby lock box. He placed his wallet in a tray with his belt and walked through the same scanners Wilson did. Once he got his wallet and belt, he joined Wilson.

They were then taken to another desk and both asked to sign a log entry at a reception desk. Elevator doors opened behind reception and a broad-shouldered agent remained inside.

"Good morning Andy."

"Good morning Ed."

They walked in and introductions were made. When the doors opened again, they walked down a very large private corridor. The building was huge. It was almost more impressive than the White House, Wilson thought. At nearly 3,000,000 square feet, J. Edgar would have liked it. Too bad he died two years before it was finished in 1974.

They stopped at another receptionist's desk and all three signed in.

Andy turned to him and said, "I'll be out here until you're finished." With that said, he turned around, sat down, and picked up a magazine.

Another large door opened into yet another smaller reception area and Wilson was asked to step inside. Ed introduced him to Sharron with two r's telling him she would take him into the Director's office. He returned to visit with Andy.

"Mr. Wilson, may I get you any coffee, a cola, or water, sir?"

"No thank you."

"The Director will be with us shortly. Please have a seat," she said motioning to leather furniture nearby.

After about ten minutes, Wilson noticed a small green light on her desk and she stood up. She smoothed her skirt, straightened her blouse and walked over to a set of large double-doors.

"Mr. Wilson, Director Jackson will see you now."

She waited until he was next to her and opened one of the two doors.

"Director, Mr. Wilson is here, sir."

"Come on in Mr. Wilson. Have a seat. Can Sharron bring you anything?"

He stood up and they shook hands.

"No sir, I'm fine, thank you."

The doors closed behind him.

"I wanted to meet you in person Mr. Wilson. May I call you Michael or Mike?"

"Mike is fine, sir."

"I wanted to meet with you, Mike, to hear personally what has been going on. When Assistant Director Joyce received the President's call last month, steps had to be taken that do not exactly embrace promotion. The Bureau has been very busy since then. You can imagine the firestorm when the FBI and CIA collide.

As a point of interest to you, there will be no notes and no recordings made. This conversation is off the record. I just hung up the phone with the President, by the way. He informed me that the Director of the CIA and seven of his Directorate have decided to seek early retirement, effective at the end of the month.

So, Mike, tell me how the series of events unfolded."

I am more curious why the face-to-face this morning, sir," he concluded. . "I don't mean to be disrespectful, but I'm sure you know as much as I do. You may even know more."

"Well, Mike, you had both agencies on high alert with the CIA operating inside the United States which as you know is a clear violation of its charter. I am not certain those that directly ordered involvement are still alive. I do not wish to talk about that. However, their people are locked up and I want them quietly prosecuted. I also don't want to talk about any files that you may or may have not seen.

"However, I want this to end here. If you have a problem, if you suspect the CIA has not stood down as ordered by this President, you are to pick up the phone and call Assistant Director Joyce. He will take any necessary steps. I am not asking.

"One last thing.

"I do not know who you work for. It was strongly suggested, implied, hinted – whatever word you would like to use – by the President before he got off the phone this morning, to leave you alone. I think his exact words to me were, "Robert, I don't want you to leave any bruises on Mike Wilson or his Annie Chavis. I like them. Make sure they enjoy the sunshine when you are done visiting."

"No one is above the law. You would do well to remember that. Please share my thoughts with your Miss Chavis."

"Yes sir, I will."

They stood up and shook hands, and the doors opened on cue behind him. Sharron was standing there. She entered as he walked out. When he passed into the next area, Andy was waiting for him.

"Let's go," Wilson said.

He led the way and Ed met them in the hallway. The three of them entered. Andy asked about Ed's wife and children while they rode down. Wilson was deep in thought. How did the Director get Chavis's name? On the upside, he did have a better understanding of who Director Jackson was. He certainly did not welcome political interference and had no time for people who sidestepped the law. Maybe that was the purpose of his meeting. He wanted Wilson to know he was not a player and was not going to be dragged into any game.

The Tahoe was waiting at the entry and both Andy and Wilson climbed in.

At the side of the White House East gate Andy got out.

"Mr. Wilson, my agent will take you to your vehicle. Our business is completed. Thank-you for your cooperation."

"Hey Andy, thanks for making things pleasant. We'll probably see each other again."

They shook hands. The agent drove past the Secret Service detail on the side of the Willard and into the underground garage. He pulled up next to the Jeep and Wilson got out.

"Wait Mr. Wilson. I have your bag."

The agent removed his quick bag from the back of a nearby Tahoe with government plates and handed it to him.

"Andy asks that you wait until you get out of the area sir, before you arm up. We're not comfortable this close proximity to the White House."

He drove out and Wilson tossed the bag into the Jeep. Just outside the beltway, he pulled over and removed the .45 from the bag. He place it at the small of his back before he walked around the Jeep checking for trackers or radio emitters of any kind. It was clean. He was starting to get that itch again. Something was bothering him. He headed out towards I-66 W for home.

The Bureau had lost three agents, one of them a bad one. The Director made it clear the matter was not over. Yet, he wanted Wilson's involvement ended.

The President wanted his involvement ended.

If it was over, he thought, why wouldn't his involvement end? Why was he being warned off? Robbie, Jeff, and Maria, three of his friends, had died. He thought it was over. Maybe that was not true.

Before he knew it, he was headed across the property to the pump. Once he gave it a push and the pad came up, he jumped in the Jeep, drove on, and dropped down below. He hurried inside. Wilson knew he would not be at ease until he got out of his new suit. It took him all of about ten minutes and after pulling on jeans and a tee, he already started to feel better.

Prince appeared and looked at him as if asking where he had been. Wilson told him what had happened while filling up his chow and water dishes. Once he saw the food, he no longer was interested the rest of Wilson's story apparently as he turned his back on him.

Wilson checked his phone to see if Doc had called. He could only hope Jill had been so confident she would prevail, that she never told anyone about the hospital or Doc. She probably figured she would tie up loose ends herself. Maybe she was embarrassed to admit she had been taken down. Not knowing troubled him. Time would answer that question.

11. TRANSFER OF WEALTH

Wilson powered up the phone. Doc had called.

Prince did what he did best and disappeared somewhere. More and more Wilson found himself being like Gus and having no concerns about intruders. He was beginning to appreciate the level of security Gus had put in place. He grabbed his quick bag and walked out the front door, headed to the Jeep pad. Walking would give him more time to think and was good exercise.

After he brought the Jeep to the surface, he jumped in and headed to Doc's. Summertime weather in Virginia always was nice. The humidity was what sucked, though today it was comfortable.

He arrived at Doc's and Mae came out to the porch as Wilson climbed out of the Jeep. She gave him a big hug and handed him a lemonade.

"Have a seat on the porch, Mike. Doc is coming out with some stuff."

"Thanks Mae."

Doc came out and smiled. He gave Wilson a fatherly hug.

"The town's attorney, Edward Helland, paid us a visit. The last time we saw Mr. Helland was when the town was first formed and Gus wanted to be sure we knew that everyone would be taken care of, in the event of his death. We instantly liked Mr. Helland. By the way, we always knew Gus was special, but we did not know he was a friend of the President's. When some folks saw the funeral, they were hoping Mr. Helland would stop by and speak with us. He also brought you a large sheaf of papers and made me promise to give them to you. Here they are."

"Thanks Doc. We should have spoken about this sooner. Gus affected all our lives. I realize you knew him longer than I did, but in hindsight, I feel he was like a grandfather to me."

"He spoke very highly of you Mike. Gus was a man that seldom praised other men unless he thought they deserved it. When he came to address the town before he left last, he told us you would be taking his place if he did not come back. He said you would make that known at your own pace and swore us to secrecy. He reminded us that he never asked much of us except to believe in him. He said we could safely transfer that belief to you. He told us to give you that much. As you can imagine, we were all troubled. We loved Gus and didn't want him going away. I suspected he was sick. He began to keep his distance from me and had started coughing as if his lungs were failing. I didn't realize he had cancer. That damn smoking will do it all the time."

"Doc, I'll contact Mr. Helland tomorrow and have more information for you then. In the short term, know that you guys will be just fine. The town should be too. I need to get going."

He climbed into the Jeep and placed the large envelope of papers on the floor before heading back home. He needed to put his life back together. It seemed like he had lost control of so much of it.

When he got back, he took the paperwork inside and made a sandwich. Grabbing a cold Bud Light, Wilson sat down to eat lunch and read. The reading took him over an hour and he read it one more time to absorb all of it.

From what he could gather, Gus had made him a billionaire. Wilson now owned all this property outright including the large ranch that bordered the U.S. Forest. It was a lot to take in. He didn't find any restrictions or instructions. There was nothing telling him what he had to do or what he could not do. Gus died after placing all his trust in him. The last page was a note from Mr. Helland asking Wilson to call him right away.

He sat back to think before he made the call. Could he do the same thing when he got old or sick? Gus had bestowed two huge responsibilities. One was wealth and the other was protecting America, even if it was from its own government. Would he find someone one day? Would he find someone he had this much confidence in, to do the same?

He removed his smartphone from his bag, put the SIM chip into it and called Edward Helland.

"This is Edward Helland, how may I help you?"

"Mr. Helland this is Michael Wilson."

"Mr. Wilson can we meet tomorrow, say 10 AM? I have to fly out in the afternoon and I want to get all of Gus' business resolved before I do that."

"Yes sir. 10 AM sounds good. Where are you located?"

"Do you know where the Watergate building is in D.C.?"

"I have never been there, but I'm confident I can find it."

"Come to the Virginia Avenue building. You will find my offices on the 11th floor. See you at 10 AM. Thank-you, Mr. Wilson."

He hung up the phone. Wilson decided to check his drop box and see if there were any new messages. He went downstairs and powered up the computer. He had forgotten about Tracy. Still, there was nothing new from her. He sent her a message and told her he would look for her tomorrow at 3-PM at Audie's residence and signed off.

Tomorrow, he would get the big stuff out of the way and maybe take a vacation.

When darkness came, Prince returned and Wilson grilled a couple steaks and baked two potatoes. He cut the larger steak up for Prince and put it into his bowl. He refilled his water dish and set it down. Prince looked at him and Wilson believed Prince somehow knew he was holding back a baked potato. He cut it in half to cool and set it on the floor next to the bowls.

Eating his steak reminded Wilson of the night he had stopped at the Keg. A lot had happened since then. He had been shot twice and some of his friends had died. He met Gus and it changed his life. He would never want for money and he inherited an entire town to support. Why did Gus want to create a idyllic town? And how did Gus know Mike was the "one"?

Wilson wished Gus were still here. He needed to sit down with Gus, discuss all that had happened, and ask what he thought. He wanted to ask him why the President and the FBI would tell him to end his involvement if it was already over.

When he thought about that, Wilson realized he already knew the answer. It wasn't. Somewhere, part of this was continuing. He just did not know in what form or where or maybe he would know why.

By the time he got up from the table, Prince had vanished as always. He cleaned up, admired his day's handiwork, and poured myself some Jack Daniels. Good ol' Number 7. Sometimes it cleared the cobwebs; sometimes it wet a dry throat, and sometimes it just helped make the day go away. He was not sure which of the three he was looking for this evening.

Time had passed and it was getting late. He pulled out the digital display to summon Prince but he could already see his diamond moving this way. They were starting to think alike. He tapped it twice and put it back into his picture frame. When Prince arrived, Wilson praised him and gave him a hug. He growled a little. He was not big on hugs. Wilson sent him on patrol and locked up for the night.

In the morning sunlight entered from a skylight. He got out of bed and pulled the sheets tight. Looking up, he realized the skylight had a steel power cover. He might have closed it when he went to bed had he known that. Getting up with the sun was starting to become a habit.

After shaving and showering, he got dressed in his jeans and tee shirt. He pulled on a pair of boots and walked out into the hall. There lay Prince sleeping. Prince half-opened his eyes to tell him, he knew Wilson was there before closing them again. He wondered. Where did Prince sleep and when? He was always working or at least it seemed like it.

Wilson made them breakfast. He found some oatmeal for himself and put some dog chow into Prince's bowl as well as giving him a fresh bowl of water. They looked at each other for a minute and Wilson said, "That's right friend, you do not get steak every day."

Thinking of that, he was going to have to make a grocery run in the near future.

He pulled out the quick bag and removed all his weapons. He spent the next two hours cleaning and oiling them. He checked firing pins, safeties, and all the loads before repacking them except the .45 he left out to carry into D.C. He pulled out one of Gus's Pendleton shirts and loosely buttoned it to conceal the .45 at the small of his back.

By 10 AM, he was parking in the lot of the Watergate Office complex. There was a lot of history and Presidential interference involved with Watergate. Most people thought of President Nixon when they heard the name. They didn't know that President Kennedy played a role in its construction while President nor that the Vatican was one of the original owners. If only the walls could talk. It was a little known seat of power where Senators still gathered today to talk in secret.

He took the elevator to the 11th floor and found Helland, LLC on a large door. When he entered, he was quite surprised. His office occupied all 16,000 square feet of the top floor. The view was tremendous. There were cubicles, office staff, and apparently other attorney offices. The furnishings were quite lavish.

"May I help you?" asked the closest receptionist.

"Yes, Mike Wilson to see Mr. Helland."

"Miss Jones will take care of you from here Mr. Wilson,"

Miss Jones stood up and reached out for his hand and introduced herself. "Hello Mr. Wilson. Welcome to Mr. Helland's office. I am Marianne Jones."

"Meeting you is my pleasure Miss Jones."

"May I get you some coffee or something else?" she asked.

"I seldom drink coffee, but thank you."

"Well then, let's not keep Mr. Helland waiting, shall we?" She moved over to two double doors behind her and opened them while announcing him.

Wilson walked inside to find Edward Helland was about 55-years old. Behind him was a picture of himself, presumably his wife and two teen-aged children. They shook hands.

"Miss Jones, will you leave us alone and please see we are not disturbed until I tell you different? Thank you."

She smiled at both of them and walked out shutting the doors behind her

"Your office is easy on a man's eyes Mr. Helland."

"Yes, well I try not to even shop, as women say, or I would lose not only my family, but everything I have worked for my entire life. My wife you see, recruits, interviews, hires and manages my staff, including Miss Jones. I could not help notice your gaze though, Mr. Wilson. I am sure it was not lost on her either. Shall we get down to business? We have a lot to go over."

"Before we get started Mr. Helland, I'd like to ask your qualifications."

"Let me make something perfectly clear, Mr. Wilson. I am not your attorney at this moment in time. I am General Gus Hokold's attorney. Once all the matters at hand are attended to, and all the 't's crossed as they say, you may retain me should you choose to do so – and should I chose to represent you.

For the record, I attended Harvard Law and graduated with honors. I was number one in my class. The General sponsored me all the way through school and I repaid him by handling all his business. I mean all of it. My firm employees twenty-five of the brightest attorneys on the East Coast and we all work for one client. And, Mr. Wilson, I don't owe anyone any favors except him."

He rolled up his sleeves and they spent the next three hours poring over documents, records, and bank accounts. Gus had vast holdings that required experts to manage. He even had a home in Europe. Most of his earnings were the result of software that he invented and sold to the government and allies from a blind trust. Did Wilson wish to keep everything? Did he intend to retain Helland LLC or did he have his own attorneys? Did he want to liquidate anything? The questions went on and on. The last audit revealed Gus – and now, Wilson – was worth 27.8 billion dollars. He was beginning to understand that being very wealthy was a business of its own.

Lastly, Mr. Helland handed him a slip of paper with an address and stated he would find a safe deposit box key in Gus' library.

"I have spent the better portion of my law career representing the General, Mr. Wilson. You are free to make your own decisions. Mind you, I will not stand idly by if I see you violate his trust. I admit there is little I can do and I don't have the resources of wealth you do. Nonetheless, I owe Gus Hokold my loyalty."

He picked up his phone and asked someone to step inside. Marianne opened the door.

"Miss Jones, please bring the paperwork for transfer and disposition, will you?" he asked. "Also, ask Teri and Lori to step in as witnesses."

Marianne returned followed by two other women. In one hand she held a notary stamp; in the other hand she carried a large stack of papers held together with one giant clip.

The two men signed and counter-signed until each page had several initials and signatures. It was like buying a house.

"Please make two copies and bring Mr. Wilson one right away, will you, Miss Jones?" The three left and closed the doors.

"Is there anything else today, Mr. Wilson?"

"Yes, I want to retain you. I am willing to keep the arrangements the same as Gus had. I need you to over-see everything. I will require your complete discretion, no questions asked for services I may need, the same as Gus, and we are going to call each other by our first names. Do we have an agreement?"

He leaned back in his chair and gave this some thought before reaching for his phone.

"Miss Jones, draw up the General's client agreement for Mr. Wilson, will you? All wording is to remain the same, and all numbers are to remain the same. Change the names only please. We will be representing Mr. Wilson from now on in Gus' place. Bring that in when you bring in a copy of the other. We will need it notarized as well so ask Lori and Teri to step in one more time."

"My firm will represent you with the same secrecy and ferocity as we did Gus. My faith and belief in you is solely based on the General's. He vouched for you. You may call me Edward. However, I will call you Mr. Wilson. That will be the agreement."

Wilson laughed and said, "Okay, Edward." Mr. Helland smiled and they shook hands. They spoke about the estate over the next half-hour until everyone returned once more. Helland asked him to complete a personal form that listed his preferences for many things including food and relaxations, clothing size, weaponry favorites and a contact method for his most trusted friend. He paused, before completing this part of the paperwork.

"Why do you need all this personal information?"

"We are here to serve you Mr. Wilson. There might be times when you will require me or my staff for support or assistance. You are the most important person to our firm. We will put things in place and have things ready for you from time to time without you having to ask. It will also allow us to respond quickly to a request if we have inventory on hand or know where we can locate it wherever you may be travelling. It's useful to better serve you – trust me."

Wilson completed filling out several pages including Annie's contact. When everything was signed and he had a copy of each, Wilson stood up. So did Edward.

"Do I have to take this paperwork with me or can I keep it here?"

"I suggest you hold at least one copy of everything we do. Put it all in a safe deposit box."

They shook hands and he left his office.

At 3-PM, he drove into Arlington Cemetery by showing a pass to the guard at the gate. He parked his Jeep about 100-yards from Audie Murphy's gravesite and walked back to pay his respects.

Tracy walked by with her ball cap pulled down and headed up to the amphitheater. Wilson soon followed and sat down.

"Hey, Tracy. Sorry I did not get back to you sooner. I didn't have access to a computer and was flat on my back for a while."

"We picked up on some of your dust-ups, Mike. You were lucky. Very lucky. Chavis was too. My boss has always been a fan of you two and he said there was a lot of scuttlebutt about bringing Chavis in especially after two agency people were shot a mile out. Not many people can make that shot, back-to-back.

Anyway, I do not want to talk about that. I have to report any conversations. Not personal you understand."

"No problem from me, Tracy or I would let you know upfront. What was it you wanted to tell me? Why did you reach out?"

"Chavis already jumped on it so I figured you guys already discussed it. That's why I didn't bother you a second time."

"I haven't been in contact with Annie in a few weeks. I don't even think she's still in the Country, is she?"

"Mike, we're off the record here – now."

Tracy continued, "Chavis is in Italy. The Admiral of the Navy had her moved and turned over to civilians there. He's keeping an eye on her."

"Who are you talking about Tracy?

"Your girl from the hospital ship."

"Wait. You are saying Maria is alive?"

"It's what I think, Mike, yes. Look, it's just me helping you two. You know how it is. You worked there for a while. If you have a team on something, you get everything. I still have to do my real job, you know? I got bits and pieces for you when I had a moment here and there."

"I didn't mean to be critical. I know. I am surprised you picked up what you did. When was this, the transmission you got?"

"We picked up on it not long after that thing occurred at your condo. I think you had just come back from Camp David, but I am not asking. The Admiral of the Navy received a Presidential order to sedate her and relocate her from the USS Comfort to the NAS Gaeta in Italy. She was turned over to somebody off base afterwards by a Naval Security detail.

Chavis is there now and said she would see what she could find out. That was her last message."

"Does anyone know besides you and Annie?" he asked.

"If you mean, is the NSA involved, no. No one seems to be interested. All of that died down. Heck, I thought the two of you knew and Chavis was taking over protecting her. No?"

"Look Tracy. When you file your report today, just keep it kind of a check-in thing. No details and do not mention Chavis okay?"

"Mike, I need my job. I'll hold out as long as possible but having a pension and staying out of prison is everything."

"Okay, just do this. If you have to break confidence, let me know first, all right? Let me know first if anyone is asking. I promise you'll be taken care of."

Tracy stood up and pulled her cap down even lower, "You make me think you work for the President sometimes," she said with a laugh. "I love you like a brother Mike. Be careful." She walked back down the hill.

He had lied to him. The President had looked him right in the eye and lied. If he did not, someone was abusing his authority. Moreover, what about Jackson? Did the FBI know? The CIA?

There are no coincidences. Wilson stood up and made a decision. He stopped at a phone store and bought a prepaid cell phone. He called Edward Helland's office and Marianne Jones answered his direct line.

"This is Mike Wilson, is Edward available?"

"Sorry, no he's not. He took an afternoon flight."

"Marianne, I need you to charter a jet, but not in my name. I don't want anyone to know I'm leaving the country. It has to be big enough to fly from D.C. to Italy and I don't care what it costs. I have to leave as soon as you find one. Does this number show up on your screen?"

"Yes, it does Mr. Wilson."

"Call me when it is ready."

****

Annie Chavis had learned from the locals that no one wanted to speak about the villa. They seemed to have some allegiance to the owner, but she could not get a grasp of why. Finally, an older woman directed her to the village priest. Father Starcelli knew everything and everyone she said.

Chavis planned to visit him in the morning. It was getting late.

* * *

Wilson jumped in the Jeep and hurried out of Arlington. Damn it, damn it. He wished he had brought his quick bag. Traffic was heavy. The workday was over and people were starting to commute home. It took him forever to get to the Jeep pad. He jumped out and turned the pump before jumping back on to head down. In the tunnel he ran when his disposable store phone rang. It was Marianne.

"Mr. Wilson I found you two pilots and a stewardess. There will be a new Beech jet 400A chartered in the firm's name standing by at Dulles. They need to fuel it and stock the kitchen. That will take over an hour I am told. The pilot needs to file a flight plan. He is asking for the Italian city you want to fly into."

"Tell him to pick the nearest place he can land that is near Naval Air Station Gaeta."

"How far away are you?"

"I'm at least ninety minutes away with traffic. I will get there as soon as possible. And thanks."

He hung up. Prince was lying by his quick bag. Wilson told him he would be back when he could and filled up four bowls with chow and four bowls with water before leaving. If he was gone longer, Prince would have to put those hunting skills to work he had heard about, or go up to the town. He ran out and jumped into the Jeep.

The drive to Dulles was dreadful. He arrived there almost two hours after he had spoken with Marianne. Wilson found the office for the private charters, parked his Jeep and went inside.

At the counter, he presented his ID and asked where his jet was. He explained he was not familiar with the procedure, apologized, but said he in a hurry. The counterman made a couple of calls and told him to wait down the hall by the door to the tarmac, pointing behind him.

"Excuse me, are you Mr. Wilson?"

He turned around to find a very pretty redhead. This was his day to meet them he guessed.

"Yes, I am."

"Hello, I am your stewardess, Karen Murtagh. Follow me and we will see what we need to do to get going. I understand you are in a bit of a hurry."

They walked out across the tarmac for about two hundred feet and into a hanger containing what looked like a brand new jet. She asked him to follow her up the stairs and take any seat. He climbed up and into the rich man's way of life. The seating was more opulent than any living room or den he had ever been in. It also smelled new.

He grabbed a swivel seat at a large circular table in the back and set his quick bag across from him.

Once they were airborne, Karen brought a whiskey and set it down.

"Mr. Wilson do you have any questions about your jet or our flight, sir?"

"Does it show? I mean the fact that this is all new to me. Do I look like a fish out of water?"

She laughed. Her eyes sparkled and he noticed she was not wearing a ring.

"A little. I enjoy flying charters. People know what they want and expect to have it in their hands when they want it. You, on the other hand, are more curious about your surroundings. You also show an interest in people."

"Speaking of people, Karen, when do you and the pilots get to eat? Is that something you take care of?"

"I do. My passengers are first and the crew is second. The crew is supposed to eat prior to flight and they snack during if they choose to."

"What kind of rules apply to passengers, to me? I've flown in different planes, some military, but this is my first time in a private jet."

"Aside from civility, remembering the Captain is in charge of the plane, the rest of the rules are what you dictate. You are free to stand up, walk in what space there is, or even sleep. If you plan on using the bedroom, please let me know what time to wake you or how much time you need to shower and dress before landing."

"There's a shower and bedroom on this jet?"

"There is in the rear, yes sir. Inside it you will find a small bathroom with an even smaller shower," she said and laughed again.

"I don't think I am tired enough to try sleeping in a bed on a plane for the first time in my life. Can I stretch out on the couch?"

"It's your jet Mr. Wilson."

"Call me Mike."

"Your assistant, Marianne? She made a point that I was to remain attentive, but formal. 'All business' was her directive. I think I want to keep her on my good side. Off the plane, well, that is my territory, Mr. Wilson. We can talk then about calling you Mike."

"Marianne is no fun. I think I'm going to stretch out on the couch for a while."

He lay down and the .45 pushed into his back. He sat up and pulled it out.

Karen looked at it and said, "You don't have to hijack your own plane you know. Hand me that and I'll put it on top of your bag in the cupboard."

"Sorry – it's habit. Are you familiar with firearms?"

"Both my dad and brother are police officers. They made it a point to teach me how to handle guns."

Without further questions, she took his .45 and put it away. He closed his eyes. Somewhere over the Atlantic the cabin lights were dimmed, and Karen covered him with a blanket.

* * *

The Catholic Parish was at least one hundred and fifty years old. The stained glass, the plaster, and the beautiful timbers looked like someone had recently restored them. After walking around the outside, Annie entered the church rectory and sat down in the rear. The sun had been up for a couple hours and he hoped to catch the priest early. She was soon rewarded. An elderly priest approached.

"Can I help you?" the priest asked.

"Father, I am not a Catholic. I am no longer sure I even have faith, but I need your help. Will you help me?"

"I don't think our heavenly Father cares if you are Catholic as much as he cares if you have faith. Of course the Bishop would not like it for me to say so, but I am an old priest. What is it you need?"

"Father, there is a friend of mine who is staying in the large yellow villa on the hill above your church. I am concerned for her safety. Do you know if the people that own it are good people or bad people that own it?"

He paused quite a while and sighed.

"If you have a moment, please come into my office."

He got up and walked towards the front of the church stopping to genuflect in front of Christ at the alter. From there he walked into the hallway and turned right.

Chavis got up and walked past the alter without following the old Priest's example. She found the Priest's office and sat down.

"The villa you are asking about … might I know your name and a little more about your interest?" the priest asked.

"Father, my name is Annie Chavis. I have a friend that was badly treated by some people and hospitalized. When she was released, some people brought her here without telling her family. I want to be sure she is safe. I think we would all feel better if we knew who owned the villa."

"The owner is a very private gentleman. He gives generously to the village and to our church. He visits once a year. One time, I asked him why he would own such a lovely piece of property and not live here year around. You know what he said?

He said he was busy keeping the world sane. Sane.

We would share a glass of wine at night; sometimes we would drink here and sometimes we would drink on his balcony. Overtime our conversations centered more and more on faith. I could tell he ached inside. He did not have family. A man like that had much to teach someone."

Chavis spoke, "You said 'had' Father. Where is he now?"

* * *

"Mr. Wilson? Mr. Wilson? Time to wake up. We will be landing in about forty-five minutes." It was Karen shaking him awake.

He stood up, stretched and walked down to the bedroom. He used the bathroom and found all the toiletries he had forgotten to bring. All his brands were in the cabinet. He decided to take a quick shower. By the time he finished, he felt alive once more. He carried his dirty tee shirt in his hand and walked out to get a clean one from his bag.

"Mr. Wilson if you just tell me what you need, I'll be glad to get it for you," Karen said.

"I need a clean shirt from my bag, but I don't allow anyone to get inside it so I'll do it myself, thank you."

"You have a closet here and drawers full of your clothing," Karen said, pointing to a side of the hallway.

This must be what Edward was talking about, the need to know his personal preferences. He grabbed a clean tee from a drawer and pulled it on. After pulling on his boots and brushing his hair, he was ready to get on the ground. He put the .45 inside his quick bag.

"Mr. Wilson, you won't get that bag through customs, not with a gun or guns. Everyone, including private flights get the welcome treatment."

"I didn't think about that. I am used to flying military hops. Any suggestions?"

"There is no alternative. You cannot just bring guns into Italy. You will have to leave them on the plane."

He winked at her and said, "We'll see." He pulled out a satellite phone and called from the bedroom. It didn't matter if anyone knew now since he was physically here. He told them where he would be landing and that he wanted an embassy car to bring one large forty-eight inch diplomatic bag to him. They would be at least an hour, he was told.

Soon Wilson was asked to prepare for landing. They rolled onto the ground and pulled into a large hangar. The pilots came out in the cabin and introduced themselves. The Captain, Brian Lawrence, had completed a recent stint in the military flying officers from base to base in the United States. His co-pilot, Captain Roger Vold had been an F-18 fighter pilot in Iraq.

Brian asked how long they would be here. He told him he didn't know at this time. Certainly, they would be here overnight, but he suspected it would be more like two to three days. Maybe longer. Brian and Roger wanted to see some of the village before renting a car to head into Rome if there was time. Wilson said to go ahead and asked for his cell number.

"One thing I need, Brian. Will you fuel the jet and have it ready to go at a moment's notice? Also, I need to make sure the galley will feed at least three more passengers on the return flight. If you will make arrangements to do all this before you leave today, I would appreciate it."

"Yes sir, will do. Just to let you know, Rome is an hour's drive time. We'll need at least an hour to get back when you are ready."

Wilson turned to Karen, "So, what are your plans?"

"Well, if we are going to be here at least overnight, I'll find a place to stay and check out the village. If you plan to stay longer, I might head into Rome."

"Can I get your number? This way I'll have the pilots and yours so I'll know everyone has been told when it is flaps-up time."

She smiled and gave him her number. All three men exited the plane.

An Embassy car arrived. He told the driver, Rudolpho Luigi, to climb inside the jet and zip the embassy bag around a bag. His stewardess would show him where it was. Rudolpho brought it out under the eyes of two custom agents that were arriving to inspect the plane. He placed it into his trunk and waited. Wilson told him he needed to go inside and walk through customs.

When he came out, Karen was walking over to the taxis.

"Hey, Karen. Wait, let me give you a lift."

She turned and looked around. He came around the embassy Cadillac and opened its door for her. She laughed and walked over.

"Aren't you a surprise, Mike?"

"Where can we drop you?"

She walked over. Rudolpho took her bag and put it in the trunk.

"I need to find a place to stay. Maybe your driver knows where I can stay cheaply that's safe."

He asked Rudolpho to take them to a nice hotel where Karen would be safe. He took them to the Villa Irlanda Grand Hotel. It was in old town near the beach and was beautiful. Obviously, it was a four or five-star.

"Look Mike, I can't afford this and I'm not sharing a room if that's what you are thinking."

"Hey, you'll have your own room. My company will pay for it and I doubt I will see you much. How can you resist that deal? You're free to do what you want."

She looked at him for a moment and said, "As long as we're clear. I've never been to Italy before and I just kind of wanted to do it on my own."

They got out and Rudolpho handed the staff her bag. He removed Wilson's quick bag from the embassy bag in the trunk and handed it to him. Wilson tipped him a $100 bill.

The Villa Grand lived up to its name. He handed the front desk a credit card and told them he would pay for Miss Murtaugh's account. She checked in and went upstairs to look at her room. Meanwhile, Wilson asked for a corner suite and carried his own bag upstairs. Inside, he found a loose panel in the sitting room and hid it behind that.

It was too bad he was here on business. The beachfront was beautiful. He removed the compact .22 with the silencer and put it in his boot holster before going out.

Wilson planned to locate the villa and scope it out by daylight. Then, he needed to track Annie down and get their heads together.

* * *

Father Starcelli crossed himself and kissed his Rosary before answering. "I didn't know he was such an important man. He never spoke of such things. I saw on TV your President buried him at Arlington. He was a General, our Gus."

"And now, Father, who owns it now?"

221

"I have no idea. I can only hope it is someone that is kind and will take care of our village like Gus has."

"Thank you Father."

Chavis left the church and walked back to her room at the B&B Il Vecchio E Il Mare. It was located by the Marina. She checked the Do Not Disturb sign on her room and the hair on it was still there. Inside, Chavis removed her bag from behind the closet where she had kicked a panel out. She pulled out a satellite phone and called Tracy's cell number. It went to voicemail. Chavis said, "Hey, it's me. I want to return the gift. Please call me."

When Tracy played it back, she would understand that Chavis meant she was to have Wilson call her. Things were starting to break. When Wilson got the call, he would start calling on the half-hour until they spoke.

Chavis repacked her bag and hid it behind the broken panel in the closet. She checked her watch and decided she had time for a sandwich.

* * *

Father Starcelli had not moved from behind his desk since Chavis left. He knew what he must do but he did not want to set something in motion he would regret later. He opened up the cupboard where he kept the wine. Under Gus' glass was a piece of paper with a phone number on it. He had promised long ago in return for the work on the church to call. He was supposed to call if anyone asked about Gus or the Villa he owned.

With heavy fingers, Father Starcelli dialed the number to the United States. It rang three times and a woman answered stating she was someone's assistant. He did not recognize the name.

"This is Father Starcelli, in Italy. Hello."

"Hello Father, my name is Marianne. How can I help you?"

"I know our Gus is gone but I made him a promise to call this number if anyone was asking about the villa. There's a woman here asking."

Marianne wrote down all the information Father Starcelli gave her, including a description of Chavis. After she hung up, she dialed a number and passed the information on. Both of them had now done what was asked of them.

12. A SURPRISE

Wilson hiked up to the address he had memorized and saw a beautiful yellow villa with white trim. The grounds were meticulously maintained and there were no line of sight problems between the walls and the house. The second floor balcony that looked out over the harbor was 3/4 wrapped around the house. The glass had a tint that he recognized as bulletproof. There were large standing floodlights on the corners of the grounds. Someone had taken great care to make it difficult to penetrate. There was probably an elaborate alarm system as well. The next thing would be to count guards or staff. Right now he didn't see anyone. No cars were parked outside. The villa appeared to have a five-car garage so they might be hidden from view.

He would return tonight. Something still bothered him but he could not quite see it yet. He started walking back to the Grand.

* * *

Chavis went back upstairs in the B&B and waited for Wilson to call. It probably was too soon, but she gave it five minutes before putting things away. She wanted to walk down to the marina and scope out boats in case she needed to leave via the water. She went downstairs and out the backdoor.

On the street, Wilson came around the corner just as Chavis emerged down the block. At least it looked like Chavis. She still had that walk, that sway. He may not have seen it in years, but he knew it when he saw it. Wilson jogged to close the gap.

"Hey Annie!" he hollered.

Chavis turned around and waved. She waited for Wilson to close the distance.

"How'd you get here so soon Wilson?"

"I charted a jet."

"Thanks for this Annie; thanks for keeping an eye on Maria. What is the status at the villa? I just came from there and it's more secure than it looks I am betting."

"Did you get my message?" asked Chavis.

"No. I just picked up a message from Tracy yesterday that was a week old. We met and she told me you were over here protecting Maria. You can imagine my surprise after the President told me she was dead."

"I never heard the dead part. Tracy told me they were moving her from a Navy hospital ship and flying her to Italy. I thought that was a bit over the top so I decided to check it out myself. Do you think the same folks have her?"

"I have no idea. We need to scope it out tonight and come up with a plan to get in and get her out. Any idea who owns it?" Wilson asked.

"Here's a wakeup call for you. According to the village priest, an American General named Gus that is a friend of your boss. The General died and Father Starcelli has no idea who owns it now."

Wilson broke out into a smile.

"What – why are you smiling? What do you know?"

"Annie you hit gold. I think. I have some of the pieces of the puzzle. Gus is Gus Hokold. He is the friend that willed me his property. I was at Camp David when I learned he died of cancer. He never said he was sick. And, this place? I knew he owned other property but I never saw it listed. I guess I was reading too fast and just didn't care."

"What do you mean you were reading too fast? Have you been checking out this guy? Is he the guy behind all this?"

"No, at least I don't think so. I think he probably helped orchestrate saving her life. Before we hit that place, we need to know more. I have a contact that knew Gus really well. The problem is I am not sure how to get a hold of him, but he has an assistant and she will. Have you eaten?"

"Matter of fact, I just had a sandwich, but I could go for a drink. Where are you staying at?"

"I'm over at the Villa Grand."

"Must be nice to be rich. There's a pub not far from there called Rendez Vous. Let's meet there in one hour. I want to scope out the boats in case we need to make our exit on the water. See you soon."

Wilson turned and headed back to the Grand. If she only knew how rich he was and how well he knew Gus. He had never kept secrets from Annie Chavis but now was not the time to tell her. He walked into the lobby and took the elevator upstairs to make the call. He removed his bag from under the sink and pulled out the satellite phone. He called Marianne. It would be almost midnight but he trusted the direct line to Edward would be switched to someone at night.

"This is Mr. Helland's executive assistant, Marianne, how may I help you?"

"Hey Marianne, this is Mike, Mike Wilson. I need some information."

"Go ahead Mr. Wilson, tell me what you need."

"I need to know if Gus listed a home in Gaeta, Italy and if so, if I own it. Where did Mr. Helland fly to and why?"

"Mr. Helland's itinerary is not sharable, Mr. Wilson. I will need to go into the office to access the safe for your property listings. Call me back in 30-minutes. I live at Watergate so I can get dressed and walk over to the office building."

"Can you at least tell me if Mr. Helland is in Italy?"

"No, I can't." She hung up the phone.

About thirty minutes later, he called her back. She answered and told him the address of the property Gus previously owned in Gaeta. It was in fact now his. He thanked her and hung up. He grabbed his bag and put things away. It was time to meet Chavis and get Maria out.

At the rendezvous he had downed one Bud Light before she joined him.

She sauntered in. "Thirsty are we? Couldn't wait? So, tell me what you know."

"You're looking at the owner of the villa. Gus left it to me."

"Do you have any idea what that property is worth? Let's kick the door and toss out whoever you want."

He laughed. It was vintage Chavis.

"Technically, I own it. I doubt the paperwork has gone through yet so it might take a few weeks or a month."

"I'm a patient girl, Michael Wilson," she laughed.

"First, let's get Maria out. We need to get her to a place where she's safe, let her get her wits together, and then see if any sharks are in the water."

Chavis had visited the villa a couple times at night and during the day. It appeared there was only one woman. The same woman came and went. If there was anyone else, she was very good at keeping the other one out of sight. Her movements made Annie think she was a professional.

"I think the gal with Maria might be pulling double duty as a nurse and bodyguard. It is just hard to tell. And I have no idea who she is working for. Could she be working for you? Could she be on our side? Hell, you didn't even know you owned the freakin place until an hour ago."

"No idea, Annie, but I want Maria out of there."

"Well first Mike, we need to plan. We need a plan to get her out, a place to put her, and a way to get her there," Annie said, "Let's slow the train down. As far as we know, they do not know we are here or if she is working for you. I say we scope it out tonight, sleep on it and decide over breakfast if we walk in in broad daylight or hit and run under darkness tomorrow night and make a run for it."

"Okay. I'll call my crew and give them a heads-up," he said.

"No offense Wilson, but do you know these guys well enough? I mean what if we are tipping our hand to the CIA? Let's have Tracy check them out for us while we sleep."

"None taken, you're right. Let's have a good dinner tonight and I'll tell you a story about my new wealth. Afterwards, we'll go up the hill and we can get a night vision on the villa."

"That sounds good, except Wilson? I don't want to know how rich you are. I am happy just knowing you. You can damn well buy my dinner though and pay to get me somewhere when this is over. Fair enough?"

"Fair enough.

Annie grabbed a napkin and pen from a waitress and sketched out a plan to flee from the Marina if necessary. They would need to front a deposit to the owner of a speedboat. The owner would run them out to a nearby island and a helicopter would take them from there to a 120-foot yacht that they could lease to get them back to the East coast. She would need a full twenty-four hours to set it in motion, but they could leave right away for the island where a house was and stay there overnight.

They cleared the bar and chose to get some exercise walking around the village. As they walked past the villa, they did not see any activity. Blackout shades covered all the glass except the front of the deck, which was obscured from ground view. They would need a boat and a sniper's scope to see in that way. Wilson was tempted just to walk up to the door and knock.

Hi, I am the new owner. Can I come in and see my house? However, he did not.

Both of them went back to their rooms to double-check their equipment. He called Tracy and left her three names of "his cousins" to check out, telling her he thought they were charlatans. Hopefully, she would run a background on them and let him know his crew was A-Okay.

He called Karen's room, but she was out. He left a message telling her he wasn't bothering her, but just checking in to see if she was having fun. After he hung up, he thought maybe he shouldn't even have done that. Technically, she was his employee. Having employees sucked. There was a lot to being rich he still had to learn about.

Masaniello's was packed. They didn't have reservations, but slipping the maître d' $100 got them outside on the deck. The menu was great but neither one of them were very hungry. They settled on a bottle of wine and lobster. It was delicious. The company was even better.

They changed in their rooms and met outside, in front of the Grand. They walked around the corner and up the hill where Chavis pointed out Father Starcelli's church, Our Lady Mother of God. Even at night, it appeared extraordinary considering how old it was.

Finally, they reached the area of the Villa. The exterior was lit up as much like a bright small parking lot. There was nowhere to hide. Chavis handed him her binoculars. He could not see inside. All the windows were covered. Assessing the situation was difficult.

"See what I mean," Chavis said. "It's strange."

"Maybe we should just knock on the door in the morning. Do you have any water spray? I was thinking we could at least see if there are lasers running across the fence line, before we leave."

Chavis passed him an eight-ounce water aerosol can. He crawled down next to the fence and sprayed upwards. Red lasers lit up like the Fourth of July. The alarm system was elaborate.

"Let's go, I've seen enough," he said.

"Hey Wilson, cheer up. We'll figure something out in the morning."

She was right, of course. He was going to stay up and then call Tracy to catch her first thing when she got through the gates at NSA. If his crew were clear, he would call them in the morning and give them the heads-up. Chavis and he would make the snatch and fly out.

They parted in front of the Grand with a hug and he walked inside. Passing the bar, Wilson noticed Karen sitting by herself eating dinner. He walked in and sat down.

"Buy a stranger a drink?" he asked.

"I might. You kept your word. You have not bothered me. I'm not sure if that is something to brag about on my part or not though."

"I told you I had nothing but good intentions. Speaking of phone calls, do you mind if I run up to my room and check my messages? I'll be right back."

"No, I started off by myself and if you don't come back, I'll cry alone." She smiled.

"I'll be right back."

He took the elevator and ran down the hall to his room. Inside, he removed his bag and the sat phone. He dialed Tracy and lucked out. She had to come in early. The relatives were okay people. Be nice she said.

Wilson got back to the bar in record time and Karen appeared surprised.

"Now, about that drink?" he said.

He signaled the waiter and asked for a Jack on the rocks.

They clicked glasses and he signaled for another round.

"Thanks for not pressuring me or giving me a bad time. But could you just a little, you know, flirt … to make me feel good?"

"Yes, but then you'd say no, and it would be awkward for both of us." They laughed.

"Well, one never knows sailor. Besides, the chase is half the fun, isn't it?"

"Well I learned long ago not to disagree with a woman if I were trying to get her to do something."

"And what is it, that you would be trying to get a woman to do?"

"I am thinking of a way out, why don't you tell me about yourself," he said.

"I grew up in Portland, Oregon, a product of two hippies. My mom and dad were Jerry Garcia fans and life moved along at a come-as-you-are pace. My mom taught school and my dad was a Safeway store manager. Every year we drove down to Ashland for the Shakespearean festival.

When I got in high school, I discovered boys or they discovered me. I decided I wanted to move out; I wanted freedom. I moved to my aunt's in Rhode Island and she helped me get into Brown University. While there, I began thinking about flying and well, here I am.

I started flying for United Airlines. One day I met a man named Dennis Earick who was seated in First Class. He was flying home to Texas. He asked if I ever considered flying private jets, charter jets. I had not but he assured me the money was good and the time off even better.

If I built a reputation, I could fly when I wanted he told me. It sounded pretty good and he helped by getting me my first job. I have been doing this for a couple years now. How about you?"

"My life is kind of boring probably compared to yours. I work for a boss that is demanding and expects me to be available twenty-four hours a day, seven days a week. I am sort of a federal officer. I travel a lot. The pay is good, but the life is not good for a girlfriend or a wife. I am just not around that much. Sometimes I get injured and get laid up. Welcome to my world."

She looked over at Wilson and said, "I'd like you to be in my world tonight."

He laughed and said, "I'd like to be in your world too, but it's taken you four drinks to invite me. Plus, Karen, I have somebody

They left. In the elevator, she looked up and gave him a big smile whispering, "thanks" into his ear.

The doors opened to her floor and she stepped out. She put both hands on his chest and gently walked him backwards into the elevator. She raised up on her toes, kissed his nose, and said, "Next time, big boy." She walked back out and he heard her laughing as the doors closed.

He shook his head and laughed too.

13. THE CONTRACT

When the elevator opened on his floor, he found Edward Helland waiting in a wingback chair near his door. Helland stood up and said, "We need to talk, Mr. Wilson." Wilson looked at his watch and it was 2-AM.

When you are a new billionaire and your attorney is waiting up for you at 2 AM and says "we need to talk" it's never good news. He did not expect his to be any different.

"C'mon in Edward," he said unlocking his door. "Can I pour you a drink?"

"Yes, I will have one. Scotch if you have it, neat."

Wilson found a bottle of fifteen year old Macallan and poured it into a crystal glass. He poured his favorite on the rocks too, and they sat down. Wilson raised his glass and offered a toast to Gus. Helland returned it.

"Well, to what do I owe the visit?" Wilson asked him.

"I understand you and a woman named Annie Chavis are making inquiries about the villa on the hill, the one you own."

"We are, yes. How does that concern you?"

"I wanted to let you know Gus promised sanctuary for the girl in that house. There is a large trust fund attached to the house for that reason until she is well enough to leave. It is paying for all related expenses including security. I flew over to make sure everything was or is as it should be before telling you since Gus had died. Gus dealt with all kinds of tragedies and secrets. I only involved myself if he asked. I didn't want you to stumble into or get involved in something you needn't be a part of. Gus carried a heavy load, if you know what I mean."

He stood up, chugged his Scotch, and turned to leave.

"Edward? I will always do the right thing. Do you know what I do or who I work for?"

"No, I don't, on both counts. Nor do I need to unless you need legal advice or counsel. Remember, I am here not only to give you legal advice, but I am here to give counsel. Tonight, this morning, I am giving counsel.

Goodnight, Mr. Wilson"

He shut the door behind him.

Had Wilson not had the drinks, he probably would not have slept as well as he did. However, he was not rested when he woke up. His body let him know it in the morning. He called over to the B&B where Chavis was and invited her for breakfast. Since B&B's in Italy did not serve the large American breakfasts, she was more than happy to join him. He chambered a round in his .45 and put it at the small of his back. He also took the satellite phone.

They ate in the restaurant of the Villa Grand. Chavis looked at him and smiled. He had missed that smile.

"Had a few drinks last night, did you Wilson?"

"I did. I also had a visit from my attorney at 2-AM concerning the villa. You were right. The woman on the premise is the only security. Maria is already in my protection in a sense."

"Do others know she's here? I mean the assholes in the CIA or anyone else that would want to hurt her?" Chavis asked.

"No, I don't think so. And I don't know that I could put her anywhere else where she would be safer."

He sighed.

"Wilson, do you want me to check the security out today? Do you want me to line up some physical security? Tell me what you need me to do."

"After we're done here, let's walk up and introduce ourselves at the villa. We will both check out the security and interview the lady handling the security. I want to talk to Maria and see what she wants to do, too."

He shared with Annie what Helland said. Frankly, he was out of ideas until they paid a site visit. It was then that Karen entered the dining room. Flashing a big smile, she came over to their table.

"Good morning Mr. Wilson. Did you sleep well?"

"Good morning Karen. Karen, meet Annie Chavis. Chavis this is Karen, my flight attendant."

They said hi and shook hands. They also gave each other an appraising.

"I would invite you to eat with us, but as you can see we are finished and just leaving. I apologize. I am thinking we will fly out late this afternoon. I'll call you or one of the pilots and pass the word when I know for sure."

"Yes sir. Enjoy your day. Nice to meet you Annie," she said and she went over to a table that looked out onto the courtyard.

Chavis said, "Your flight attendant? You have your own flight attendant? Karen is a knockout. Tell me you were not drinking with her. I saw something pass between the two of you."

"Okay, I won't tell you I didn't have a few drinks with her. But that was all." Annie just laughed.

They finished eating and walked up the hill. They had to stop at the exterior wall and press the intercom to make contact.

"Yes, who is it?"

"It's Michael Wilson, the villa owner. I'd like to come in and visit with you."

"Wait there Mr. Wilson. I will come to you."

In about five minutes, she arrived at the gate. Her appearance was impeccable. She appeared to be about thirty, and carried herself with confidence. In her right hand, she made no attempt to hide a Beretta 92SF. They also knew each other. It was Rita, the same Rita who treated my first gunshot wound.

"I am leasing this property for the remainder of the year, Mr. Wilson."

"May I come in Rita?"

"No, you may not. Please leave or at the very least, I will sound the Claxton horn alarms and ask the Italian police to arrest you. Push forward and I will shoot you."

She produced a small remote that had been in her left hand.

"Will you allow me to make a phone call to a mutual friend? You can verify my identification with him."

"You may call anyone you wish Mr. Wilson so long as you walk away as I requested." She walked sideways moving back from the gate while keeping the Beretta handy. She disappeared from sight.

"Wait a minute. You two know each other?" asked Chavis. "Jesus, Wilson. Is there any female involved in this that you don't know? No wonder you need my help." This time she didn't laugh.

He dialed his direct number for Helland. Marianne answered on the 4th ring.

"This is Mr. Edward Helland's personal line. I am Marianne, his assistant, how may I help you?"

"Marianne, this is Mike Wilson. I spoke to Edward hours ago at my hotel. Now I am at the villa, my villa. I want to get inside to visit with the security, but she needs verification of whom I am. Can you or Edward call her and have her invite me inside?"

"Mr. Helland called me after he met with you. I will make the call. Please call me back in ten minutes." She hung up.

He waited ten minutes and called back.

"It's Mike."

"Go ahead,Mr. Wilson, approach the gate. Security will allow you and only you inside, but she may keep a weapon trained on you. She makes the rules while under contract."

"Thanks Marianne. I owe you dinner."

"You can buy me lunch if we talk business maybe. Mr. Helland will not allow dinner." She laughed and disconnected.

"Annie, you have to wait outside the gate. I can't get you in, but I don't want you to leave."

"Your house – your rules."

"I was told that the security made the rules and if I wanted in, I would have to comply – sorry."

They both walked down and Wilson pressed the buzzer again.

"Yes?"

"Rita, its Michael Wilson again."

"I'll be right up."

Rita appeared once again with gun in hand walking up to the gate.

"Mr. Wilson. I'm going to open the gate with a remote from where I stand. Only you are to come in. If anyone else – anyone – comes through the gate besides you I will shoot them. Are we clear?"

"Perfectly," he responded.

The gate clicked open and he stepped in. He turned around and swung it closed. Chavis said she would wait. Wilson turned back around and walked towards Rita.

"When you get to the second gate, I want you to stop and turn around. Place your hands on the wall there, step away until you are literally holding yourself up with your hands like a pushup. Then, Mr. Wilson, spread your feet 4-feet. I want 4-feet in between them."

"I should tell you Rita, I am carrying."

"I would be surprised if you weren't. Please do as I stated."

Once he got into the position she asked him to, she opened the wrought iron gate. She stepped out and put the gun to his head.

"That's a bit drastic, don't you think?" he asked.

She didn't reply, but quickly found and removed his .45. She stepped back and he heard her eject the clip and the chambered round onto the pavement. Out of the corner of his eye she tossed the gun onto the grass. She removed the .22 from his boot that he had forgotten about. Then she frisked him twice, both times thoroughly and stepped back.

"Walk around the corner and carefully step up the stairs. Stop at the door."

She followed holding the gun to her side, keeping her distance from him. They stopped at the front door and she used a very odd-cut large key to unlock what obviously was a solid steel door. She pushed it open and stepped aside.

"Go ahead Mr. Wilson, walk inside. Be careful. I don't want you to fall on your face unless I put you there myself."

They entered the house and he walked down the entryway into a beautiful living room. It had an even more spectacular view of Gaeta and the ocean. He could see security construction built-in and around every window. What he could see of the hallways was that each one had a dropping fire cover panel. This home was over-built to be a fortress.

"Wait here Mr. Wilson and I'll go and get our guest."

While he waited, he thought maybe this was the best place for Maria after all. He was even more impressed with Rita the second time around. She took no chances. But this time he had a lot more questions for her than when they first met.

"Hi Mike."

He turned around and was speechless. Her make-up was impeccable and someone had done their best to cover her eyes from whatever beatings she had suffered. He could see they had hurt her badly. He could see it in her eyes. A couple fingertips had synthetic skin on the tips to accelerate healing. One arm had a liquid bandage near the elbow. However, it was her inner being that had been damaged the most.

"Hello, Maria. I have looked for you when I got your message. I really did. It took me a long time to find you. I am so sorry for what they did to you." He wanted to add that he had killed all of them, but he wasn't so sure yet.

She lowered her head and began to cry softly. Wilson stepped in and took her into his arms.

Rita spoke, "Please be gentle. She's hurt pretty bad."

He hugged her tenderly and looked into her eyes. He had so many questions. She looked like she was about to collapse in his arms and he nodded to Rita who led her away.

When Rita returned, Wilson let at least three or four seconds pass before he spoke. He didn't want to regret any thing he was about to say.

"Why didn't you tell me?"

"Mr. Wilson, I don't work for you. I really don't know you."

"I admire your attention to detail Rita, but make no mistake that this is my home and I am the one paying for the security."

"No disrespect meant, Mr. Wilson. When I have a signed contract, I adhere to it. Moreover, I work only for my client or clients whose name is on the contract. Yours is not one of them."

"Well, then I suggest you call the name on your contract and put them on the phone. I want to talk to them. I am not leaving."

"Mr. Wilson, the reason why I am here is because you couldn't or didn't protect her. I can and I will. Maria is badly hurt, more emotional than physical. She is one of those people that is just a gentle soul and not prepared for evil if you know what I mean. I will bring her back; I will breathe life back into her, trust me. It is what I do. It is one of the best things I do."

"I wasn't even in the States when they grabbed her, Rita. She is my neighbor. As soon as I found out, I began looking for her. I have been shot three times trying to find her. You of all people should know and I have lost two friends. I never gave up. I saved her and then lost her again. I don't want to leave her.

"Yes, well, that's what I said isn't it? You couldn't protect her and then you lost her again. I won't, and you are leaving

242

right now." She stood up, moved away while speaking and holding her Beretta at her side.

"Look, …Rita … will you let her call me when she feels like it? Will you let me fly over to see her when she's ready?"

"Mr. Wilson, she is not my prisoner. She is my client. If you hear from her, it is because she wanted to call you. If she extends an invitation to you, you will be welcomed. When she is ready to leave here in my opinion, you can come get her if that is what she wants."

"One last thing. Will you take my calls and give me updates?"

"No, I will not. I don't work for you. I told you that."

He didn't respond back. Rita was correct on so many levels. He hadn't exactly been there when Maria needed help. He believed she had died and showed up making demands when he had no authority. He admired Rita. The stance she took and how protective she was spoke volumes about her. As he walked out he thought about how Rita had showed up on his doorstep. She treated him and was willing to give her life to protect him. He guessed he owed her too.

He stepped outside and moved around the corner to put his .45 back together. He picked up the clip and single round from the pavement Rita ejected earlier and chambered it before pushing the .45 into the small of his back. Then, he picked up his .22 under her watchful eye and slid it into his boot.

At the last gate, Wilson turned around and said, "Thank you Rita for what you are doing. Thank you again for taking good care of me."

"You're welcome," she said and the gate locked as she pushed it tight before backing away.

Chavis had been listening and observing all of this with her arms folded.

"That Rita would shoot you in a minute if you climbed back over the wall. She has one job to do and she's not losing sight of it. I kind of like her. She reminds me of me. Even I have wanted to shoot you sometimes. C'mon Wilson. Buy me a drink and you can bring me up to speed".

They walked down the hill in silence.

14. TIME TO GO HOME

He ordered a Jack Daniels on the rocks and a martini for Annie. The last hour really had blown him for a loop. What a dick he was. Here he was feeling sorry for himself. Of the three women currently in his life, one was savagely attacked, one was willing to kill him to protect her client, and the other, and the most important – Annie – he treated her as if they were still buddies in the Corps. It was time to go home. He needed to get his head clear and get centered once more. More importantly, right now, he was thinking he wanted to become "that guy" to one of them.

Wilson explained to Annie how Rita was sent to treat his wound and protect him until he recovered. He hadn't realized then how good she really was; nor how serious she took her assignment. He told her how Maria looked, their short conversation, and how things were left.

"Sounds to me Wilson that unless you have something more for your neighbor in there, you should let things go. I think she's in good hands. If you want, set it up and I'll check back on her from time to time. I'm in no hurry to get back to America.

If not, I think I want you to drop me off in Dublin. I have always wanted to go there. How about that? Can you do that for me, Wilson? I was thinking you might be good for a loan or two. Maybe you should come with me, take a vacation. You should be happy now, but you seem down in the dumps. Why is that?"

"I really need to get home Annie. I want to ask my boss why he lied or find out who lied to him."

"Oh, I don't think that's it Michael. I have known you too long. You could pick up a satellite phone, get a secure line to the man himself and ask that question. You are thinking about something, I believe that. I just believe that is not the biggest thing on your mind."

She stood up, gave him a kiss on the cheek and walked out the door.

He left some money on the table and ran after her.

"Annie, wait."

She turned around and he saw a smile on her face he had not seen since she stood in his doorway after coming home to help. She looked beautiful, but then anytime he looked for more than a minute at Annie Chavis, she always looked beautiful to him.

"I'll fly you to Ireland. I'll buy you a house."

"Are you telling me Mike that you're ready to settle down?"

"Not yet, Annie, I can't yet. I just can't."

One trait Annie always had even when she was angry or disappointed with Wilson is that she laughed. Wilson could only detect the truth in her eyes. He loved her for it. She laughed now, but her eyes said more and they both knew it.

"You can't buy me a house then, but you can give me a ride on that jet of yours." She turned and walked away.

Wilson called Brian and told him to get the jet ready. They were heading to Ireland and then home.

Chavis called Rudy and he brought the embassy car out to pick up both of them and helped get them checked out. He expedited both of them through the officials and had them on board the jet within an hour. Wilson still gave him a $100 tip.

"Wilson, I'm impressed. Are you chartering this or do you own this thing," Chavis asked while grabbing a recliner.

"You know I'm not sure. Marianne would know."

"Who's Marianne again? Oh yeah, the assistant. You're going to need me around even more to protect you once these babes find out you're rich."

Karen brought out a Bud Light for me and smiled at Chavis. "It's nice to see you again, Miss Chavis. What can I get you to drink?"

"If you make a good Martini, I'd love one, thank you."

"Mr. Wilson, can I bring you anything else, anything at all?" she asked with a twinkle in her eye.

"No thanks, Karen. I am happy for now. Did the pilots tell you we are heading to Ireland?"

"Yes, they did. I have never been there before. I hope we will have a couple day layover."

"Actually we are just letting Annie off and refueling before heading home."

"I guess I'll have to see it another time." She produced two menus and returned in minutes with Annie's Martini.

"I'm telling you Wilson, that one has eyes for you."

"Shut up. When did you start drinking Martini's anyway?"

"Once we left the Marines Wilson, I started to look around and consider what's next for me.

I began to see the world differently. I met a few girls that had never been in the service. They rounded me out. I became more tolerable and worked at blending in. We lived in the same apartment complex and would meet in the evenings for a glass of wine and talk about our day. When I knew my money was running out, one of them was kind enough to get me a job at a travel agency. Then one of my friends got married and that made me want to have the same thing, a life, children, and a home. A few weeks later, I got your message and well, here I am."

Karen brought them new drinks and a plate of gulf shrimp with spicy mustard and a plate of mini-filet sandwiches with bleu cheese and onion jam.

Mike listened intently as Annie described a life that he wondered about.

"Annie, I have often wondered where you were, what you were doing, and if I would ever see you again. I'm sorry for putting you back into action."

"Mike, I will always be available for you, anytime, anywhere. You know that. And I know I can always count on you. This was almost like old times."

They landed in Dublin. Brian had radioed ahead for the embassy car to meet the jet at Wilson's request. He wanted Chavis to be able to get her quick bag in the country and not encounter any problems with her guns or the substantial cash he had quietly put inside it.

The jet pulled into the hangar and dropped the stairs as the embassy car pulled alongside. Chavis walked down the stairs with him behind her.

"Thanks Annie again for being there when I really needed you. Thank you for coming home and helping me out. I thought I could handle it and get Maria back safely. When I heard Tracy had picked up the transfer chatter I let it get my hopes up again. Seeing her again made me want revenge, but I think you already got it for me."

"Mike Wilson, how many girls would rush home to help their best guy rescue another woman? I am your right hand. I am the air that you breathe. I am everything to you. You may not know it, but I do." She laughed and turned to face him. She never looked more beautiful than any other moment to him, since he had known her.

He walked down the last few stairs and joined her on the ground. He gave her a big hug, handing her a large embassy bag containing her quick bag. He felt like she was waiting for him to say something back. He could not. It was difficult to even return her smile. He was leaving his best friend, a friend he had not seen in years, and might not for many more years again. He turned around and jogged back up as the driver opened the car door for her. At the top of the stairs, he heard the door shut, the motor start up, and the car drive away until there was only silence.

"Karen, pour me a Jack on the rocks," he said as he entered the cabin. "Tell Brian as soon as we are fueled and he is ready, I'd like to get going. I have a wolf to see when I get home."

"Yes sir."

She returned with his drink and left him to sulk. Forty-five minutes later, they were up in the air headed for the States.

"Here's another drink, sir," Karen said handing him a second Jack.

"How did you know I wanted one?"

"With your permission, Mr. Wilson? Any man that looks at a woman the way you did and then turns around and flies off is going to need a lot more where that came from." She turned and headed into the galley.

END

About The Author

Stanley Mowre is a former United States Marine having served honorably and recognized with meritorious promotions. Prior to leaving the Marines, Stanley was offered a CIA contract job which he declined due to its nature and his wanting to return home.

Upon his return, he graduated college with a degree in Criminal Justice and spent a career both as a Homicide and Patrol Supervisor in Northwest Law Enforcement. He received one medal and 44-commendations before retiring after 23-years. It was during this time Stanley was 1 of 100 invited guests to the White House, by President Ronald Reagan.

Stanley currently resides in Scottsdale, Arizona with his wife and their two Labradors, Zeus and Huck.

Made in the USA
Coppell, TX
02 August 2021

59850578R00152